D0429491

MY LIFE IN DIORAMAS

by
TARA ALTEBRANDO

Illustrated by T.L. BONADDIO

RP | KIDS
PHILADELPHIA • LONDON

Books published by Running Press are available at special discounts for bulk purchases in
the United States by corporations, institutions, and other organizations. For more
information, please contact the Special Markets Department at the Perseus Books Group,
2300 Chestnut Street, Suite 200, Philadelphia, PA 19103, or call (800) 810-4145, ext. 5000,
or e-mail special.markets@perseusbooks.com.

ISBN 978-0-7624-5681-9
Library of Congress Control Number: 2014949682

E-book ISBN 978-0-7624-5682-6

9   8   7   6   5   4   3   2   1
Digit on the right indicates the number of this printing

Cover and interior design by T.L. Bonaddio
Edited by Lisa Cheng
Typography: Museo Sans, Museo Slab, Bahiana, Helvetica Neue,
Emmascript, Extreme, and Archer

Published by Running Press Kids
An Imprint of Running Press Book Publishers
A Member of the Perseus Books Group
2300 Chestnut Street
Philadelphia, PA 19103–4371

Visit us on the web!
www.runningpress.com/rpkids

FOR ELLIE AND VIOLET. AGAIN.

In fact, I now fear you will never let me dedicate a book to anyone else.

1.

"Come on!" I said. "Come *on!*"

The school bus groaned to a halt in front of Big Red, which was what everybody called my house, because it was big and you guessed it. I got up and bolted down the aisle, throwing my backpack onto one shoulder and calling out, "See ya!" to Stella and Naveen and anyone else who was listening, and "Thanks" to our driver, Gus. Then I jumped down onto the gravel driveway and went through the gate of the white picket fence, which we always left open, and up the three steps to the front porch and through the front door, which had an anchor knocker that no one ever used. I went straight into the old bathroom and was careful to close and lock the door because otherwise it opened on its own, which meant the mailman could see you through the window next to the front door.

A stinkbug sat perched on top of the T.P. roll so I shrieked, took off my shoe, whacked it, and yelled, "URRRRRGH!" Then I scooped it into the trash with a big wad of paper. I flushed just as the stinkbug, true to its name, started to make the room smell sour.

Back in the foyer, I grabbed my backpack and hurried through the dining room and into the kitchen, where I stopped to pet our very old, very big, very white dog, Angus, who was lying in a heap by the kitchen table, where my parents were sitting.

"How's my favorite daughter?" my mom asked.

"Still your *only* daughter!" I said.

I went through the doorway into the newer section of the house, then upstairs and across the loft that looked down onto the kitchen. I said, "Oh, and Dad, I killed a stinkbug and it's stinking up the bathroom trash."

"Kate," my father moaned. "You're not supposed to kill them!"

"I know," I said. "But I was peeing and I panicked!"

I went into my room, where I put my backpack on my desk chair. Lately my mother had been making a fuss about my leaving stuff everywhere and how she wasn't my servant and on and on. I was making an effort.

I ran back downstairs and through the kitchen and out the screen door in the dining room to the back porch, where I tapped my mother's wind chimes to wake their sounds, then took the stairs down to the yard *slowly*, like I had ever since

I'd fallen down them when I was seven and needed seven stitches on my forehead. Past the pear tree and around the vegetable garden toward the barn, the stream was loud—the last snow of the season had finally melted last week—and it sounded excited. Like even *it* knew that the kittens were here.

* * *

For social studies homework, we were supposed to make a shoebox diorama of a scene from our life. I'd thought about doing a little scene of me sitting on the old metal bench down by the stream, where I liked to race boats or look for frogs and tiny fish. But I was really hoping that Pants had come through for me because a diorama of me and Pants and kittens in a barn would be awesome. I wasn't sure Mrs. Nagano and the rest of the class would appreciate my current first runner-up idea—a little scene of my mom and dad fighting about money at the kitchen table while Angus and I looked down from the loft.

* * *

I crossed my fingers as I dragged the old barn door open and went past my ballet barre into the part of the barn that Dad had started turning into a guesthouse a while back. I heard teeny, tiny mews as I peeked around the corner.

Pants and her one-two-three-four-*five* new kittens had made a little home for themselves in an area that had been framed out to one day be a bathroom. For a bed, they were using a piece of insulation that had fallen out of the unfinished wall.

I squealed and Pants raised her head. Realizing it was only me, she put it back down. I'd named her when I was four— her back legs were white, making it look like she was wearing pants—but she wasn't our pet. Not like Angus. She just lived in our woods and sometimes in the barn. We never fed her or anything but she did okay on her own and her kittens (or at least a few of them) probably would, too.

"Congratulations, Mama Pants," I said, then went inside to tell my parents the news.

Dad was putting down his phone and was saying to Mom, "Well, it's done. It'll go up tomorrow."

They both looked miserable when they spotted me.

"What'll go up?" I asked. If I got to work right away I could finish my diorama in time so I could still go out and scooter on the tennis court, which wasn't actually a tennis court—just a big blacktop. My parents thought it was funny to call it a tennis court but I'd never been sure why.

"Honey." My mom came and took my hand and guided me over to the table.

"Your father and I—" She paused and looked at my dad. He raised his eyebrows and she sighed and took her long hair and twisted it to fall over one shoulder. "There's no easy way to say this."

I'd imagined this a bunch of times because of all that fighting.

Drumroll, please . . .

THE DIVORCE.

Just a few nights ago, I'd climbed into bed with my headphones and phone, listened to the song that brought my parents together, and imagined how it all might end. The song's called "Semi" and my dad wrote it when he was in an indie rock back that used to play all over New York City and up and down the East Coast. They were a guitar band, but for "Semi," Dad heard a part for a violin in his head. So he'd put an ad in an arts paper and my mother, who was trying to make a living as a violinist at the time, answered and helped finish the song. She started coming to gigs to play with the band on "Semi" and pretty soon they were married. Listening to the song made me feel sad that maybe their love story was coming to an end. But that didn't explain the phone call.

"We're selling the house, Kate." My dad held my gaze.

Everything went very still.

Through the open window I heard the stream surge.

It made no sense.

We *loved* Big Red.

Everybody loved it.

Me, my parents, Angus, our relatives, my friends, my parents' friends—pretty much anybody who had ever walked through the door. This was where we had big family reunions where people pitched tents in the yard and all the cousins stayed up late watching movies on a sheet hung between two weeping willows. This was where me and Stella and Naveen spent long summer days jumping rope on the tennis court and having picnics on the little island that formed when the stream split in two during the high season.

"But why?" I asked.

"It's too much house for us," Dad said. "We need to downsize."

It was true that it was a big house for just the three of us and Angus, but that had never bothered anyone before. One of my mom's favorite jokes was that we had a "napping room," which was a guest room, of course, but she really did like to nap there.

A lot, lately, come to think of it.

"But where will we live?" I asked.

My parents passed a look back and forth.

"We're not *actually* sure," Dad said.

"We're probably moving in with your grandma and grandpa for a little while," my mom said. "I'll take a little break from work or maybe do some stuff remotely, if I can, and your dad can freelance from there. Until we can figure some things out."

My mom's parents lived about an hour away. We went to their house for dinner maybe once a month and sometimes my aunt Michelle and uncle Keith would be there with my cousins Tom and James, but . . . *living with them*?

None of this made sense.

"But this is where my friends are," I said. "Where my school is, and my dance classes and, well, everything."

If we were living an hour away, how would that even work?

"We're not happy about it either," my dad said.

"Then why are you doing it?" I asked, my voice loud.

"It's complicated, Kate." He took off his glasses, rubbed his eyes.

"Use small words." Now louder.

"We know you're upset," Mom said, "but it's no reason to be fresh."

Across the street, Troy, who'd gotten his license about a year ago, was pulling out of his family's driveway, car radio blasting.

What else was there to say or do?

Cry, maybe?

Scream?

For a second I wished they *were* getting a divorce. I felt like it would be better than this.

"So! We need to get the house ready to show." My mom got up and started to straighten the utensils in a jar marked

UTENSILS on the countertop. "And we'll need to think up some fun stuff to do when the agent is showing the place, okay? There's an open house scheduled for Sunday so we'll need to clear out."

"This can't be happening." I stormed out of the room.

"Kate!" my dad called, but I heard my mom say, "Let her go."

So I went up the new stairs and across the loft and said to them, "Oh, and by the way, Pants had kittens."

I slammed the door to my room.

Grabbing my phone and falling onto the bed, I texted Stella, **My life is over.**

She wrote back, **???**

I tapped out, **Selling Big Red**, and the words got blurry because tears were forming in my eyes. **Moving. Don't even know where.**

I couldn't even text about it anymore. I couldn't even see. I managed, **Gotta go. Bye.**

C U tmorrow, she said. **Hugs.**

A stinkbug slowly crawled out of the shoebox I'd set aside for my diorama.

2.

When Angus woke me up with a series of cool, sand-papery licks on my right hand, I was still in yesterday's clothes. But my lamp was off, so someone had come up to check on me. I could feel stiff skin and dried tears on my temples and cheeks.

So it wasn't all a bad dream.

I didn't move to get up.

What was the point?

I just lay there and watched a stinkbug inch up a windowpane.

I'd started thinking of them as the zombies of the insect world since they were so vacant seeming. They'd invaded the house through ripped screens and badly sealed doors last fall. Now that it was the last week of March and we'd had a few warm days, they were coming out of hibernation, trying to get back outside. In spite of my dad's instructions to flush them alive or escort them outside in a gently folded paper towel or tissue, my preferred method of dealing *was* actually smushing, which meant dealing with the foul odor. But it felt too early in the morning for that kind of thing, which probably explained why my parents had stopped sweeping up the dead flies that kept appearing in their room every morning. I didn't even *drink* coffee but it seemed like you should at least be able to have a cup before killing or cleaning up a bug.

Angus passed by with another bunch of licks. "Quit it."

He whimpered as he walked in a circle and settled on the braided carpet at the foot of my bed. The sloped ceilings above me looked neat but were actually pretty annoying since I couldn't make my bed without hitting my head. The room had two doors and two tiny closets, and the windows were small and opened in, like cabinet doors, which meant you couldn't put any furniture in front of them.

My room was in the old part of the house. Like *really old*. Like 1900 or before. But I loved it anyway. I'd lined the mantel of the closed-up fireplace with my collection of tiny glass-blown animals, and, somehow, the room always felt like a secret.

"Kate!" my mom called out. "The bus is going to be here in ten."

Maybe I could move some furniture, barricade myself in. My parents would have to update whatever listing they'd written to say the house came with a number of unique features, including its very own twelve-year-old girl.

I pictured my mom sitting with her coffee in the living room, feet tucked beneath her on the butterfly-patterned chair, looking out all of the massive windows facing the backyard to see if any deer or geese were going to parade through this morning. That part of the house was added on by the people who lived here before us and the vibe they were going for was obviously "ski lodge," with big knobby wooden beams everywhere you turned. Since my parents loved to ski and rock climb and hike and all that stuff, it made sense they picked this house over the other ones they looked at when I was a baby.

"Kate!" Mom called again.

"I *heard* you!" I shouted, then I got up and changed my clothes. I spotted the shoebox while I quickly, barely brushed my hair, but it was too late for a diorama.

I gave Angus a quick rub behind the ears, then grabbed my backpack and went downstairs. I took a banana from the bowl on the kitchen table and walked to the end of the driveway, aka the bus stop.

My mom appeared with her coffee on the front porch and leaned against a post. Her blue dress, the white porch, the red house, the sun shining on her long, wavy blonde hair, the steam coming off her coffee mug. It was somehow this classic American-looking scene—a photo meant for a museum, or maybe the diorama I should have made. I couldn't imagine her living anywhere else.

She called out, "We'll talk more later, honey. Okay?" Then she waved weakly.

I didn't wave back. The bus came and I got on and slid into my usual seat next to Stella.

She said, "Tell me everything."

"They're selling Big Red." It felt more real now that I was actually looking at Stella and saying those words and watching the house disappear from view. "They don't even know where we're moving to so we might move in with my grandparents for a while. Which basically means I'm going to be homeless."

"I don't get it." Stella shook her head. "Why?"

"I have no idea!"

But then I thought of all the talking about money and the envelopes coming to the house with red stamps on them that said FINAL NOTICE, and the way the whole place had started to feel more run down lately. Like the front porch paint was peeling, and the washer and dryer were, my mom had been joking, just one step up from a washboard. The dryer knob had broken off so now there was an adjustable wrench in its place and only one setting—high heat—that worked. And why hadn't my father ever finished the guesthouse, anyway?

I pushed down the lump in my throat. "I guess we can't afford it?"

Stella's eyes went wide and she said, "Stiiiinks."

Which reminded me about the stinkbug I'd forgotten to get rid of.

Great.

We were quiet for a while—both just looking out the windows. Everywhere you looked were apple trees, sometimes with pear trees thrown in just to be crazy.

Neither of my parents had straight-up, nine-to-five, Monday-to-Friday jobs and I'd always thought that was cool. My dad was a freelance graphic designer who still occasionally wrote songs. His old college roommate, Shay, was a music manager and had gotten a few of them placed on TV shows I'd never heard of and that mostly weren't on the air anymore, except for one that went into reruns. My dad got checks in the mail sometimes, but not for a ton of money.

My mother worked part-time for a local event planner, mostly organizing small conferences, regional networking dinners, or team building workshops, so that was pretty low-key, too. It meant we could do fun stuff after school, and when we had snow days or random school holidays and half days, my parents were pretty much giddy and planning some adventure. During the summer, it was almost as if neither of them worked at all. But it had never dawned on me that when they weren't working, they weren't making money. Not like Stella's dad, who drove to Poughkeepsie every morning and got on a train to New York City. Not like

Naveen's dad, who managed a bank, and mom, who was a professor at the state university in town.

I shifted in my seat and Stella said, "Oh, careful," then moved a bag she was holding by her feet so it was farther away from me. "Hey, where's your diorama?"

"Didn't do it." The empty box was still on the floor of my room. Was Angus still lying there on the rug, or had he moved to the front porch to get some sun? Had he sniffed the shoebox? Scared the stinkbug away?

"Nagano's gonna flip," Stella said.

"Considering that my whole life is ruined, that's the last thing I'm worried about." I'd never skipped any homework before, but didn't want to admit being nervous. "What does it matter anyway? Somebody could buy my house like this weekend and I won't even be around long enough to fail her class."

Stella said, "Maybe it'll take a while. You know, to find someone who wants to buy it?"

I nodded, feeling the tears start to back off.

"*I* know! If you have to, you can move in with *me* to finish out the school year."

I nodded again. "You're the best."

But it wasn't about finishing out the school year.

It was about the rest of my life.

And anyway, my parents would never go for it. Stella and I had been best friends since before we could even

remember, and our parents were friends, too. But even after all these years, Mom and Dad were still always saying things about how Stella's parents were "a little intense" and I didn't think they meant it as a compliment.

I liked the spirit of Stella's suggestion, though. I liked the idea that I wasn't totally powerless.

"Maybe I can get them to change their mind," I said.

The bus yanked to a stop in front of school. It was just one story high—red brick and windows—spread out wide on a large grassy piece of land, with a big circular drive-way in front. Some of the windows, where the lower grades were, had cutouts of flowers and other projects taped to them, which probably looked cute from the inside—mac-aroni art, no doubt—but from out here it was just clutter. I closed my eyes for a long, hard second and pictured my school in miniature, a diorama in a shoebox that I could take with me wherever I went.

"Oh man, look at Kate." Megan Tinson was one thing I would not miss if and when we moved. She was standing in the aisle. "Did you even brush your hair today?"

"Oh, what do you care," I said, and I linked my elbow around Stella's as we got off the bus.

How do you stop life from moving so fast and out of your control?

There had to be a way.

3.

"I'm disappointed, Ms. Marino," Mrs. Nagano said. "I always look forward to your projects."

I was disappointed, too. I didn't love social studies but I liked Mrs. Nagano because she treated us like people, not pesky kids. I'd really wanted to do the project. So as she walked away from my desk I said, "Wait! What if I do two dioramas by tomorrow? To make up for it?"

"I guess that'd be something." She turned to me. "Of course, even with a second diorama I'd still have to tick you down a mark for tardiness."

"I understand."

Stella and I met eyes across the room and she pretended to wipe sweat off her forehead.

I did the same back but I wasn't out of the woods, not

yet. I'd have regular homework plus everything at home to deal with and there were only so many hours in the day. And it was Thursday, which meant dance class—I'd forgotten my dance clothes. I was pretty sure I was doomed.

We were supposed to go around the room and pick a diorama to write a response to. I liked an underwater seascape I saw, with a tiny scuba diver in a pink suit and a school of fish made out of some kind of shiny gold paper hanging by invisible wire. But then I saw it was Megan's—she was always taking these spectacular vacations—so there was no way I was going to write about that one. I was impressed by the precision of a diorama that showed a family of four on the Walkway Over the Hudson—a pedestrian bridge that linked our town, Highland, with Poughkeepsie—but it was strangely lifeless and it was Sam Fitch's. If I picked that one to write about, Stella would insist that I really did have a crush on him (I didn't!) and never let me live it down.

I kept finding myself drawn back to a diorama of a bear and a shark waging battle in a shallow body of water.

I knew it had to be Naveen's diorama, so I hadn't even looked around for his name. Just last week, when we'd been sitting on the sidelines together after being eliminated from a game of elimination volleyball in Gym, he'd asked me, "Who do you think would win in a battle between a bear and a shark?"

I always tried to give smart answers to Naveen's questions. "Well, the bear could just grab the shark by the tail and throw it out of the water and that'd be that. But, hmmm. I guess the shark could just bite the bear's claws off." Then I decided, "I'm going with shark."

Naveen had started talking and talking about each animal's strengths and weaknesses, never actually answering the question himself.

As I sat down, I heard Mrs. Nagano say, "But the assignment, Naveen, to be clear, was a scene *from your life*."

"It is," he said. "It's a scene from inside my head, which is very much a part of my life."

Mrs. Nagano shook her head and smiled and moved on. Maybe Naveen would be a good person to ask for advice about how to maybe get my parents to change their mind.

On a clean sheet of paper I wrote:

The bear versus shark diorama makes me feel curious to know more about bears and sharks. It also makes me feel like there is a lot about the world that I don't know. Who would win in a competition between a bear and a shark? I honestly have no idea. But I would be excited to find out.

It wasn't the most honest answer. The truth was that the diorama made me sad about the possibility of moving because of how much I'd miss friends like Naveen. But Mrs. Nagano didn't need to know that.

"Hey, Naveen," I said, as we were walking out of class. "If

you wanted to stop someone from selling a house, what would you do?"

He faced me and crossed his arms in front of his chest and appeared to be thinking. Then he released his arms. "It would depend on why they are selling it, of course, but the most obvious way would be to stop anyone else from buying it."

"But how?" I asked, and right away, an idea came to me. "Like by making it smell bad?"

Naveen laughed. "That could work!"

"You're a genius," I said, and I almost hugged him. "Thanks!"

"You're the one who—" he called out after me, but with everyone around me talking and shouting in the hall I couldn't hear what he said.

What if I was a bear and my parents were the sharks?

Who would win then?

4.

Stella's mom picked us up after school on Mondays and Thursdays and drove us to dance class; my mom drove us home. I decided not to ask Stella's mom to stop by Big Red for my dance bag but instead had asked Stella if she had extra stuff, which she did.

Schwoo!

I did *not* feeling like "talking more" with my parents just yet.

At the studio, we got changed into leotards and footless nude tights and waited with the others—Madison, Allie, Nora, and Elizabeth—for the toddler class to come out of the back studio. Those girls could kill you with the cuteness and their tiny tap shoes! Whenever I saw them I wished my parents had started me in dance when I was younger. Three years into classes, I was in love with dancing, but a part of me still felt like I was catching up with Stella and Madison, who'd been coming here for a lifetime.

I liked the way my body felt different—more graceful—when someone told me how to move. I liked the way dancing blocked out whatever else was going on in my life.

"All right, dancers." Miss Emma appeared at the dressing room door. "Come in and have a seat. I've got some big news."

Miss Emma was a grown-up but not like my parents. She was just out of college and worked during the day at an office, doing a real job that she called "typey typey." Sometimes she went on auditions down in New York but so far the closest she'd gotten to stardom was when she auditioned for a job at a singing restaurant near Times Square—actually standing on a table, acting like it was the front of the *Titanic* and singing "My Heart Will Go On"—but she botched the waiting tables trial that came after the singing. We all decided it had been for the best. Now she must have finally gotten a real part!

"Soooo," Miss Emma said as we gathered around her in a circle. "I've been busy doing some research and paperwork and I'm *finally* ready to announce that for the first time ever, we're going to be starting a dance troupe that will compete in a statewide competition in Albany!"

Stella squealed and clapped.

Madison said, "Awesome." And Nora said, "Ohmigosh, ohmigosh."

"You, ladies, are going to Dance Nation!" Miss Emma looked around at us with wide eyes.

Stella and I had been campaigning for this for two years—ever since we'd gotten addicted to watching videos of dance competitions on YouTube. I hadn't realized Miss Emma had actually seriously been considering it.

As she started handing out packets of information, Miss Emma said, "There is the form to sign up. And an explanation of additional expenses, like registration fees and travel. And there's a parental permission slip. And all the details of the competition itself. I really hope you'll *all* do it. You're a great group, and I think we could do really well in the contemporary lyrical category if we really work our butts off these next few months."

I looked through the packet for the details of Dance Nation and found the date.

June thirteenth.

So it was official.

We could not move before then.

"Show of hands," Miss Emma said. "Who's game?"

We all raised our hands and I smiled over at Stella. I had a new, real reason to tell my parents we had to stay, but she looked at me funny.

"Excellent." Miss Emma clapped some tiny claps. "That makes things easier. Our Monday class and this one will become troupe rehearsal starting next week."

Elizabeth said, "Yay."

"Oh, and," Miss Emma said, "if any of you are interested in competing as a soloist, let me know after class. That's something we can discuss privately, though I should warn you that it can get expensive quickly, with the need to pay a choreographer and private classes to prepare."

So we all put our packets away and Miss Emma put on the song she thought we'd compete with and we finally, finally started to dance—just sort of following what she was doing and free-forming—and I started to feel strong, like I could handle anything. I'd never heard the song before but I loved it instantly. It was big and dramatic sounding, with female vocals that sounded like angels. I felt my body wake up from the tips of my toes to the top of my head as my bad mood blasted off me with each leap and turn. The energy in the room was totally different now than it had been before. We were going to get on a bus and perform on a big stage in front of hundreds of strangers and there'd be videos of us out there in the world for everyone to see.

• • •

Stella found me by the water fountain when we took a break. "Are you sure it's, you know, a good idea to sign up?" she asked.

"Are you kidding me?" I drank from the tall arch of water then swallowed. "We've been wanting this forever."

"I mean, yeah. I'm totally doing it." She looked at me hard. "But I mean, what if you move?"

"I'm going to tell my parents I have to stay for this. Or if that doesn't work, figure out how to delay things. Naveen gave me a great idea about how I can—"

"But if we all learn a routine together and you have to drop out, it might mess everything up and—"

"Everything okay?" Miss Emma appeared by the fountain.

I just stood there. How had we gone from Stella offering to let me stay at her house to finish out the school year to *this*?

"Yes, everything's fine," Stella said, then went to take a drink.

• • •

Stella and I got into the backseat together.

"How was class?" my mom asked.

"Great!" Stella said. "They're starting a dance troupe. If you sign up, you get to compete in Albany in June."

"That's exciting," Mom said, and you could hear in her voice how little she actually cared. My parents had tried to get me to play soccer and piano, and nothing had stuck but dance.

"Yes, very exciting," Stella said. "Though I doubt everyone will do it. It's a big commitment."

She looked at me. *What is her deal?* But it was a good idea to talk about how important this was to us so that my parents would postpone the move.

"Yes," my mother said. "A dance troupe is not something to be entered into lightly."

And right then, I realized that a dance competition was not going to be something that my parents would think was important enough to make them change their plans. They weren't going to get it.

At all.

Neither one of them.

I usually moved up to the front seat after we dropped Stella off, but this time I stayed put. I waited for my mom to say, "Where to, madame?"—an old joke—but she didn't. She said, "I want you to start cleaning your room tonight so it's not all left to tomorrow or Saturday."

"I need to make a diorama," I said.

"I thought that was yesterday." She turned into the drive-way at Big Red.

"It was. And I didn't do it. So I actually have to do two. Since I was late."

"Kate," she sort of whined.

"What?"

I sighed and she did, too.

"Well, go in and get started." She killed the engine and got out and closed the door.

* * *

I snapped a photo on my phone of Pants and the kittens still hanging out on that old insulation in the barn, then went upstairs in the house and grabbed my diorama shoebox and another one from the back of one of my closets. Then I went down to the room in the basement where we kept all the arts and crafts stuff.

This room had an old staircase to nowhere running up along one wall and I had a desk there. The next room, through another too-short door, was actually set up as a bar. My parents called it "the Salon" and spent a lot of Saturday nights there with friends during the winter—when it was too cold to hang out down by the fire pit. I thought it would make a cool diorama: a bar and some stools. A coal burning stove. A fluorescent Miller High Life sign, calling it "The Champagne of Beers." But it probably wouldn't make a good impression, us having a bar in the house and all.

With blue construction paper, I covered one shoebox and made what looked like a barn wall out of wooden sticks I colored red with a marker. I made cats out of cotton balls and twine. Before I could make a figure of myself, my parents called me up to dinner. I decided to at least feel them out a bit.

"I was wondering," I said, as I sat with my plate of chicken and rice. "Why now?" I was trying to sound really casual. "I just mean, like, couldn't I finish out the school year?"

My dad stopped midchew for a moment, then continued to eat.

My mother got up to fetch her water glass from the counter.

"We talked to a *bunch* of real estate agents," Dad said, "and everyone says summer is a dead zone so it has to be now for us to hopefully be set up somewhere else in time for September."

"But it's just three months," I said.

"I know," he said. "But they matter."

"Could I maybe stay with Stella?" I dared.

"Yeah, we're not doing that," my mother said, tilting her head at me. "Is this about the dance competition thing Stella was talking about?"

"No." I lied because I didn't like the tone of her voice. "I'm just wondering, what if you don't sell the house until the first week of June?" I shoveled my food in between sentences.

"Then we'll talk about *maybe* finishing out the school year," my dad said, and he gave my mother a look. "But I wouldn't get your hopes up, Kate. The house is priced to sell."

"You better get back to work on those dioramas," my mom said, when she saw my plate was cleared.

I didn't want to be around them anyway.

Back downstairs, I made a mini-me out of Play-Doh, with some black string on top of my head. Everyone always commented on my mom's blonde hair being so different from mine, which was more like my dad's, and for a second while I was making that mini-me, I was sad that I didn't need shimmering golden yarn.

My mom came in a while later, just as I was prepping my second shoebox. She stood quietly behind my chair for a minute. She looked for a second like she was going to cry or say something like "It's beautiful" or "I'm so sorry about all this," but then she just said, "Time for bed."

"But I didn't do the second one yet."

"Kate, it's late."

I was tired—bone tired—so I didn't argue any more. I just went upstairs to brush my teeth and put pajamas on. I set my alarm early for the morning so I could get up and make a second diorama.

Then I pulled out the dance troupe forms.

I grabbed a pen and filled out the registration form, then counted out some money I had stashed in my drawer from my last birthday and put it in an envelope with the form.

I sat staring at the parental permission slip a good long while.

I picked up a pen.

Just as I was about to forge my mom's signature, I paused.

I had to at least *try* to talk my parents into it.

I put it all in my dance bag and zipped it up.

Climbing into bed, I looked out the window. The sky looked like a piece of black construction paper that someone

had attacked with a tiny hole punch—so many stars.

Maybe tomorrow I'd make a diorama of me, asleep in this room.

Not for Mrs. Nagano, but just for me.

June fourteenth we could move.

Not a day before.

I drifted off trying to think of ways to make the house smell bad.

5.

Mrs. Nagano was acting pretty unimpressed on Friday—"Just put them with the others, Kate"—but I could tell from the hint of a smile on her lips that she was pleased I'd followed through. I'd managed to put the diorama of me on the scooter together over breakfast and a little bit on the bus, and also in homeroom. The worst grade she could really give me would be a 90. I mostly got 100s on the tests in her class so my final grade wouldn't be too bad.

Just yesterday I'd been thinking I wouldn't be around long enough to fail, but I had changed my thinking entirely.

I was going to stay.

With Dance Nation in the mix, I had to.

We were moving on to a new social studies unit, something about family life in different parts of the world, and

I studied the pictures in our textbook, of whole families sleeping on the floors of huts, of villages near rivers in countries I'd never heard of. Here I was, mad about the possibility of living with two measly grandparents, whose house was actually pretty nice, when there were people in the world sleeping on floors. I wasn't sure whether that made me a bad person or not.

I turned to a blank sheet in my notebook and wrote a note, then poked Naveen in the arm and passed it to him when Mrs. Nagano wasn't looking. It read, *Stuff that can make a house smell bad. Go.*

I'd made a blank numbered list, one through five.

Naveen was all poker-face. He totally looked like he was taking notes on whatever it was Mrs. Nagano was saying when he wrote something on the sheet in reply. I held out my hand but he kept on writing and writing and pausing in between. It was actually sort of annoying how long he was taking. But finally, he folded the page, and when Mrs. Nagano turned to the board again, he handed it back across the aisle.

I opened it and read:

1. Fecal matter
2. Spoiled food
3. Dead animals
4. Mildew
5. Cigarettes

Have I mentioned how awesome Naveen is?

I looked over at him and he looked at me and I mouthed the word, "Thanks."

• • •

"What are you plotting, Kate?" Naveen asked me on the way out of the room after class.

I looked around to make sure no one around us would be bothered listening to us.

"*Please* don't tell anybody," I said, "but my parents are trying to sell our house and I'm trying to stop them or at least slow things down. Significantly. There's an open house this weekend."

He seemed to be thinking hard for a second, his eyes looking up and away at a point high on the wall. "On such short notice, I'm thinking fecal."

"Gross."

"You have Angus and Pants. And your neighbor's cows? The ones you're always complaining about, with the mooing and all." He seemed mildly irritated but also amused. "I wasn't suggesting you . . . you know." He nodded toward the door of the girls' bathroom.

I was probably blushing. "Of course not."

"By the way," he said. "I liked your scooter diorama a lot. You have a way with aluminum foil."

"Thanks."

He winced a little and scratched his neck. "They're really selling Big Red?"

"Trying to," I said.

Naveen shook his head. "Where are you moving to?"

"I don't know. *They* don't know."

"Jeez."

"Yeah." I was *not* going to get emotional. "Anyway, like I said, I'm just going to try to . . . *delay* things a bit. Dance Nation is in June. If I make it to then, I'll be happy. I mean, not *happy*, but you know, I'll deal."

He scrunched up his face. "What's Dance Nation?"

"Oh, at dancing school. We're competing as a troupe for the first time. It's going to be *amazing*. We've been asking to do it for years. I seriously can't believe it's happening."

"Ah," Naveen said. "So that's why you want to stay so badly? Here I was thinking it was because of, you know, me."

"That, too," I said, and nudged him with my elbow. Then we were off to our next class, where I sat right near Stella.

"Naveen's a genius," I said.

She was drawing swirly doodles on the back of a folder. On closer inspection I saw they were the folds of the curtains of a stage, where a girl in a purple leotard stood holding a trophy.

"Can I see?" I asked, but she flipped the paper over, which was just as well.

I didn't want to talk about troupe or any of that, not if

Stella was going to get all worked up about it again. On the other side of the same page, she'd drawn the words STELLA + TRIS inside a heart. I didn't know where she got this stuff. I'd never even see her talk to Tris Culpberg.

"Just doodling," she said. "So what's this about Naveen? You're finally going to admit that you have a crush on him?"

"No. For the *gazillionth time*. Why are you so set on me having a crush on somebody anyway?"

"Because it's what we're supposed to be doing."

"According to . . . ?" I looked around the room.

"Never mind, Kate." She started to doodle another heart. "Why is Naveen a genius?"

So I explained about the fecal matter, and how I officially had a plan.

Or at least I thought I did.

Until Stella said, "I can't believe I'm going to stoop to your level, because it's totally disgusting, but how are you going to collect it? And where will you even put it?"

"I'll figure it out," I said.

I had to.

6.

Like most of the people on the planet, I liked Friday afternoons best of all.

Fridays were when my dad would whistle at five o'clock and open a beer and sit out back and ask me about my day and talk about weekend plans.

Fridays were when my mom cooked red sauce and meatballs.

Fridays were free and fun.

But when I came home, I didn't see any sauce on the stove. My dad was in the living room, looking through old records and playing "Semi" at low volume.

"Hey," I said, plopping down on the couch.

Angus came over to greet me so I petted him on his head.

"Hey." Dad turned an LP over to look at the other side.

"Where's Mom?" I listened as her sad, sad violin part kicked in while my dad sang the line, *"I'm passing that old farm again / I carry the same load as the last time."*

"Napping room," he said, and he sang along softly, *"Don't ever think of you anymore. My mind's clear as the road."*

I listened.

I petted Angus some more.

"Why did you write a song about a long-distance truck driver?" I asked.

He shook his head and smiled. "I have no idea." He was sorting records into crates and stopped for a second, then started shifting them again. "I guess I was writing about loneliness. Longing. Roads not taken. All that sort of stuff."

"But you were like twenty-five when you wrote it, weren't you?"

"Twenty-seven," he said. "Yes. And that's not too young to be lonely and longing for stuff."

Miss Emma was twenty-seven. I knew what she longed for—a boyfriend, an actual dancing gig—but my dad? It was hard to imagine. "What were you longing for?"

"I don't know." He looked up and out the window. "Love? Life?"

I saw Pants out the window, down by the tennis court, licking her front paws. Seeing her usually made me happy. But not today. "Do you still feel like that?"

"Do I feel *longing*?" he asked.

I nodded.

"Yeah, I mean. I guess. Doesn't everybody?"

I was longing for a lot of things right then. Or maybe just one thing. Power. Control over my own destiny.

My dad said, "But also, no, not really. I have you. I have your mother."

"So then what do you long for?"

"I don't know, Kate." He stopped shifting records again. "Time? The past?"

My mother's violin solo kicked in. It was hard to wrap my head around the fact that those notes, those words, had come out of the minds and bodies of the people who were now my parents. "How did you even know you could write songs?" I asked.

"I didn't," Dad said. "Until I did it."

"Hey." Mom came up the stairs, her hair all flat from sleep. Angus went over to nudge her hello and she bent to pet him.

She looked at me. "Kate, I need you to get started straightening up your room. The realtor wants minimal clutter."

Studying her—her droopy eyes, her puffy lips—I was worried she was getting sick, or already was. "Are we having spaghetti and meatballs?" I asked.

"Yeah, they're in the fridge," she said, heading into the kitchen. "I made the sauce this morning."

She left the room and the song ended and I wasn't sure why, but I felt relieved.

I went upstairs and found a mostly empty box in my closet and started packing my glass animals. Starting with the elephant first felt right since it was the first one I'd bought. I'd always hated going to garage and barn sales with my parents, looking at all the old smelly stuff, until I'd found a small gray glass elephant a few years before. After that I hadn't minded trolling through other people's junk so much because I had a mission. It had been another few weeks before I found another glass animal, a flamingo. It was mostly clear but had enough pink glass blown inside that there was no mistaking it was a flamingo. Even though I'd never actually been on a plane before, it made me want to go to the nearest airport and buy a ticket to Florida or San Diego or wherever flamingos lived. Then came the frog and the poodle and the panda, and before long I had a whole mini mantel full of them.

Packing them made me sort of sad, but I didn't want somebody to knock one over and break it during the open house. Actually, I didn't even want anyone to know they existed or to know anything about me. So after I was done, I started to stash anything that had anything to do with *me* under my bed.

(Which first required me to go down to get the vacuum so I could get rid of some dead, dried-out stinkbugs under there. Gross!)

I took photos of me and Stella off my bulletin board.

I took the ballerina print over my bed off the wall.

I even flipped over my bedspread, an elaborate paisley

pattern that I adored, to the plain orange side on the reverse.

When the room finally looked like I'd never lived there, I went downstairs.

"That was fast." My mom turned away from the stove, where she was stirring her sauce.

I took an apple slice from a bowl she had put on the table and couldn't think of the last time she'd actually gone to work. No wonder they couldn't pay their bills. "Any conferences or networking things this weekend?"

"Nope." Still stirring her sauce.

"Seems like things have been slow." I bit the apple and it was sour. She put lemon juice on them to keep them from browning, which was great when you were mentally prepared. Otherwise, not so much. "Shouldn't you be, like, asking for extra hours or something? Drumming up new business?"

She set her spoon down then crossed over to the sink to wash her hands.

"I need you to go out to the barn," she said. "Make sure those kittens haven't made a mess. And you have some old ballet shoes out there, I think. Just try to tidy."

I thought it was smart not to push on the topic of her not working very hard to save our house. I was going to take matters into my own hands, anyway.

"No problem," I said.

When she left the room, I grabbed a Ziploc bag and a spatula, shoving the bags in my hoodie pocket and sticking the spatula in the back of my jeans, just in case I got lucky and could collect some fecal matter this afternoon.

The barn was quiet and there were no signs of the kittens or any of their poop. They weren't idiots; they didn't poop where they slept. So I picked up my old ballet shoes and shoved them behind a few cans of paint on a shelf, and went out to walk around the yard. There had to be some fecal matter out there somewhere. But my first walk through the garden and along the stream turned up nothing. So I doubled back and crossed over one of the footbridges to the woods. Maybe there'd be some raccoon poop or deer droppings or anything.

No luck.

What had I become? Scouting out the yard for poop?

I ended up on the old metal bench by the pear tree, watching the stream. It was really running fast, and I closed my eyes and listened and then opened them again and watched the way the light played on the water, making the stream seem like a living breathing thing, a part of me.

A part of me worth fighting for.

I had to figure out my plan for real.

I needed exact logistics.

I needed help.

So I went inside and texted Stella and Naveen. **I need help! Operation Save Big Red summit—10am Truxton Pond.**

My mother was vacuuming the wooden ceiling beams in the living room. She shouted over the loud hum, "I thought we'd go roller-skating! On Sunday! What do you think?" She used her foot to turn off the vacuum. "Your father said he'll take Angus over to Joe's and help out with some odd job. So it'll be just us girls."

"Sounds fun." Under normal circumstances it would be, particularly for my dad, who loved to help our elderly neighbor Joe with projects, just to hear crazy old stories. "Can I ask Stella?" I asked, because I always did.

My mom looked at me for a second, turned the vacuum on, and said loudly, "Sure!"

I got roped into some vacuuming and boxing up of clutter in the living room. Then I was sent out to the back porch to stash random stuff like old candles and bug spray and gardening gloves. A slight breeze blew while I collected everything and my mother's wind chimes rang out a random, joyous melody that made me think of churches and Christmas. They were part metal and part wood with a green stone of some kind hanging from the main string. My dad had given them to my mom for her birthday a bunch of years ago, and I'd seen her blow gently on them before sitting down with her iced coffee or tea a million times. On cloudy days the green of the pendant looked like a deep emerald but on sunny days like this one, it lit up like a green sun in some faraway galaxy. Looking at it now made my heart hurt.

Before my mother could come up with any more jobs

for me, I went downstairs and started a diorama of my bedroom. I wanted to capture it as it looked before I'd stripped it of all personality—just in case I never had the chance to put my stuff back for real.

I couldn't make glass animals small enough so I just made a little mantel and bed. I colored a braided rug and tried to make Angus, this time out of cotton balls and some beige yarn. I put him at the foot of the bed and the whole thing looked so cozy that I wanted to just climb in.

When I was done, I headed for the stairs, but I heard my parents talking. My dad was saying, "We've been through difficult things before." And my mom said, "This feels different. *I* feel different, like I can't handle it."

I backed away and just stood there, outside the napping room.

Dad said, "Think you need to talk to someone?"

Mom said, "I don't know."

It wasn't normal. To have a mother who napped so much.

My dad called me up for dinner a few minutes later. "It's time for ze Italian meat-a-balz."

7.

Naveen was lying on brown grass that had just started to turn green, staring up at the sky with his knees jutting up into the air, one leg crossed over the other, when I arrived at Truxton Pond on Saturday morning. I had a basket full of supplies for my operation.

"Do I need to call an ambulance?" I asked.

"Huh?" Naveen's bike lay beside him.

I studied him. "Did you fall or get hit by a car or something?"

"Nah." He opened his eyes, sat up. "Timed my ride, though, to see how fast I could get here. Catching my breath."

I laid my own bike down next to his —careful that my supplies stayed in the basket—and took a seat beside him. When we were younger we'd often end up here—me, Naveen, Stella—just talking about nothing and picking grass to braid into shapes or studying caterpillars we'd lure onto sticks. Summers were changing, though. I already knew Naveen was doing a science camp and a Lego camp this year and I'd probably never see him at the pond, even if I wasn't already living somewhere else, which I probably would be. And there was talk of Stella going back to horse camp and starting to really get into dressage, which I pretended I thought was awesome but actually thought was kind of silly. What was the point of making horses do all that fancy footwork? Though the camp would be a good place to get my hands on some fecal matter.

"So why the summit?" Naveen asked.

"I'm having a hard time a) finding fecal matter and b) figuring out how I'm going to make the house smell bad without being caught."

Stella arrived and jumped off her bike.

"You were right," I said as she came to sit next to me. "I'm having some trouble with my plan. The open house is tomorrow at ten and I'm going roller-skating with my mom since we can't be home. So how can I make the house smell if I'm not there? Also, do you want to come skating?"

"Sure, I'll ask." Stella was winded, her cheeks flushed. It was sunny, warm. Like the first official feeling day of spring. March was being true to that whole lion and lamb thing for once.

Naveen said, "No need to get the stuff if you can't figure out where you'd put it and how. I think you'll have to do some kind of double back. Like, say you forgot your skates or something?"

"That could work," I said slowly. "So I have to hide the stinky stuff somewhere that I can grab it really fast, but then where do I put it?"

"You need to think in terms of maximum stinkage potential," Naveen said.

"Yes. Maximum."

"You know every inch of that house." Stella sounded bored. "If you can't figure it out, we're not going to be much help."

"I could hide it in the fireplace?" I said.

"Too obvious." Naveen shook his head. "They'll find it right away. Unless you're going to somehow rig it so that it's dangling down the chimney out of sight."

"Sounds complicated," I said. But I filed the idea away for later.

A couple of ducks were making lazy circles on the pond. I took a mental tour of the house room by room, like a possible buyer, then decided to focus on the living room and kitchen area, where I figured people would spend the most time. The loft over the kitchen was just outside my bedroom door. All that was up there, though, was a desk my dad used and a beanbag chair.

"My beanbag chair!" I said.

"Huh?" Naveen said.

"I can put it *in* the beanbag chair."

"Oh, man," Stella said. "I love that chair."

"Sorry." I laughed. "But there may have to be some casualties. I'll open up the stitches in the bottom of it today. And tomorrow, when I slip back into the house, I'll shove a bag of stink inside the chair."

"I have to admit," Naveen said. "I'm impressed."

"But where are you going to keep the stuff overnight?" Stella now sounded more annoyed than bored.

It had to be close to the beanbag chair. But I couldn't exactly stink up my own room.

"I've got it," I said. "I'll figure out a way to just hang the bag out my window overnight."

"I'm a little scared by how good you are at this," Stella said.

Naveen was nodding his head. "As am I, ladies. As am I. So you're all set, then."

"Mmm," I said, wincing. "Not exactly."

They waited, looking at me—Naveen eagerly, Stella skeptically—and I wondered how many more times we'd be here, the three of us, like this.

"Because now it's time to collect the stink," I said. "And I need your help."

Stella stood up and stretched. "I'm outta here."

"Don't go!" I tugged on her jeans. "You can just be the lookout, okay?"

She groaned.

"Where we headed?" Naveen said.

I took a deep breath and let out my best *moo*.

• • •

Depler's Orchard, home of the two cows—Daisy and Maisy—that mooed my family awake on sunny mornings, was our nearest next-door neighbor just up the road past the woods at the far end of our yard. Naveen suggested we stop at his place to get a tennis ball so we could pretend we were retrieving a ball we'd been playing with if we got caught. I'd brought the spatula, a couple pairs of rubber gloves, and some plastic grocery bags, which prompted Stella to say several times, "I am not going anywhere *near* any cow turd."

The house where Mr. Depler lived was set pretty far back from the road, and the cows lived in an area away from his front door. The odds were in our favor that he'd never see us. His car was in the driveway, so he was home, which was less than ideal, but there was no point in backing out now. If we got caught, we got caught. So I said, "Time's a wastin'. Come on."

Naveen and I abandoned our bikes on the side of the road, and took big strides down to the fenced-in area where the cows were hanging out, tails wagging lazily with their backs to us. It was a post fence, one you could slip through if you weren't as big as a cow. I had my eye on a huge pile of cow turd that was easily within reach. I headed for it with the spatula in hand and slid it under—so gross! It actually *squished*—and lifted some into the bag that Naveen, also wearing gloves, was holding.

"Man, that reeks," he said.

"Indeed it does. You think that's enough?" I asked, studying what was left of the pile. A few flies were hovering, buzzing.

"Should do the trick." He looked around and I almost laughed at how serious he looked, though, of course, I was pretty serious about this mission, too. "Anyway, plenty more where that came from if you need it."

One of the cows mooed and we both jumped.

While speed-walking back toward our bikes, I hurled the soiled spatula into the woods between Depler's house and ours. I couldn't imagine ever letting my mother flip an omelet with it again anyway.

Stella was already on her bike when we got close to her and she took off, calling out, "I'll text you later!"

And she was gone.

Naveen and I got on our bikes—with the bag of stink hanging off my handlebars—and rode over to Big Red.

"How am I going to get it up to my room without them noticing?" I asked. We'd stopped in the driveway.

Naveen studied my house, where my bedroom windows sat atop the porch roof. "I may not be *particularly* sporty. But even *I* can throw that high."

I considered the windows, the angle of the porch. "We only have one shot. Because if I can't catch it and it slides into the gutter and clogs it, I'm sunk."

"Not to worry," he said. "I am cool under pressure."

"You're the best." I handed over the bag of stink, leaned my bike against the front gate, and went inside.

My mom was in the kitchen, chopping something or other, and I said "Hi" as I went up to my room. I opened the window nearest the door to the loft and then backed away and closed it. I'd completely forgotten about the wasp's nest out there. My dad was supposed to call a guy to get rid of it but he kept putting it off. I went to the other one, the one I usually kept open a crack on warm nights, since it was closer to my bed. Tonight, it would be shut for sure.

I opened the window and popped out the screen and set it aside and knelt down, hanging out as far as it felt safe. "Ready?" I called out.

"Ready." Naveen took a few sort of running steps and hurled the bag up at me.

I caught it, barely, by the ties of the bag.

"Yes!" Naveen pumped his fist in the air.

"You're the best!" I said.

"Good luck." He got back on his bike. "Keep me posted!"

I watched as he rode off. Was a crush supposed to feel like this? With Naveen, I could be myself in a way I wasn't with anyone else, not even Stella. But I was pretty sure that was just a special kind of friendship and that a crush was supposed to be different. Naveen waved from the corner where he turned toward home.

8.

"Whatcha doing?" my dad said. I was "reading" in my beanbag chair. He'd come up, on my mother's orders, to tidy the desk, which looked like it had been attacked by wolves.

"Just reading." I turned a page to make it seem official. Was my mother ever going to leave the kitchen and let me get on with it?

My dad basically shoved everything that was on top of the desk into a drawer, moved a lamp a few inches, and stepped back, impressed with himself. "Can it wait?" he asked me. "I could use your help out in the shed."

Right then my mother went into the laundry room, so I said, "Can I just finish this chapter?"

"Sure." He looked tired and sort of sad.

"I'll be out in five minutes?"

"Great."

As soon as he left, I got up and flipped the beanbag over and cut through a few stiches on the bottom seam. I was pretty sure I'd be able to sew it closed again, no problem, if it ever recovered from the stink. I put the scissors back in my room and went out back, adrenaline pumping through me.

My dad was standing outside the shed, both doors wide open, scratching his head. I went to his side and took in the view. Skis and snowboards and a boccie set and a croquet set and the badminton net and more, all crammed in there. Behind them—pushed up awkwardly against the back wall— were my old pink plastic table and chairs. The curtains my mom and I had made together were faded from the sun.

"Remember when this was your clubhouse?" my dad said.

"I do." I just hadn't thought about it in ages.

"I'm not really sure what your mom expects me to do with this stuff."

I shrugged. I wasn't about to give my father any brilliant ideas on how to make this shed more appealing to people. "Seriously," I said. "It's a shed."

"Exactly!" He closed the doors and latched the hinge.

But when he turned to go, I opened the doors again and took another look. My cousin Ellen and I had spent one after-noon out here, making dresses out of construction paper and modeling them over our swimsuits. And one night, my dad and I camped out here, or tried to, until I got scared and we gave up and went up to Big Red instead. I used to sit on the edge of the doorway, watching my parents play croquet with their friends while I slurped an ice pop. I thought I had outgrown that pink desk, those flowery curtains. Now I regretted ever feeling that.

I usually spent some time on Saturdays at the ballet barre in the barn, practicing pliés and stretching to keep myself limber between classes, but today I just wasn't in the mood. All this stuff about dance troupe competing was really exciting. But it was sort of a new thing to stress about. And Stella's attitude wasn't helping. Anyway, she'd see. I'd postpone the sale just long enough and make it to Dance Nation and everything would be awesome.

I went upstairs and texted Stella. **Skating?**

She wrote back, **Affirmative.**

I shouted down to my mom from the loft. "What time are we going skating? Stella's coming."

"Tell her we'll pick her up at ten."

"Hey, Mom?"

She looked up at me from the kitchen.

"You *could* just drop us off if you want."

"Thanks, Kate." She huffed and looked away. "That's thoughtful."

"I didn't mean it like that."

"I thought we'd do something together, just us two, is all." She was sautéeing onions. Angus was curled up near where she stood.

I sort of felt bad, but not really. This whole forced family fun during open house idea bugged me. "I can cancel," I called down.

"Never mind," she said. "Have you cleaned up the crafts room?"

I didn't even answer. I just walked downstairs.

But I didn't clean up.

Instead, I found another shoebox.

I lined the walls with cream-colored paper and cut blue rectangles for windows. I found some flowery paper and cut little curtain shapes, then made a small pink table and chairs. I started to make me and my cousin Ellen, dressed in tiny paper dresses. I missed her and my other cousins and my aunts and uncles. Did any of them know we were selling Big Red?

I propped the mini-me and mini-Ellen up on the chairs and left the room.

9.

Xanadu or roller derby? was Stella's first text in the morning.

I'd introduced Stella to *Xanadu* a few years ago. My mother said it was her absolute favorite movie ever when she was little, and since then Stella and I had spent a number of sleepovers making fun of the clothes, the music, and the plot—where a roller-skating goddess pops out of a mural and basically inspires a failing painter to turn an old movie theater into a roller rink. I sort of loved it, too, in all its totally outdated bizarreness.

So today, I picked *Xanadu*.

I was feeling more like trying to skate my way out of my life and into some other magical realm than I felt like "AlterKate-r," my roller-derby persona. Why we felt the need to dress up whenever we went roller-skating, I have no idea.

I threw on some tights, some pink leg warmers, and a white flowing dress with big sleeves that Stella and I had found at a secondhand shop in town. Then I took the leg warmers off. Maybe I'd come back for those as part of my double back? I had a feeling my mother wasn't going to let me leave the house without my skates so I needed a fallback plan.

Downstairs, a bright-eyed, middle-aged woman with curly red hair stood by the oven, holding a sheet of frozen pieces of cookie dough. "Hello there," she said.

"Who are you?"

"I'm Bernadette." She opened the oven door and slid the sheet in, seeming so at home that anyone might have taken her for an aunt. "The realtor. And you must be Kate."

"What's up with the cookies?" I said.

"We want the house to smell homey."

So she was, clearly, my enemy.

"People really fall for that?" I asked.

"Yes."

I walked past her and into the dining room, where my parents were clearing stuff off the table in a frenzy.

Bernadette followed me and said, "It's okay for it to look like people live here. You don't have to go crazy. The place looks great. I'm feeling confident."

"Oh good." My mom was wearing leggings and an over-size denim button-down shirt. She grabbed her car keys. "Then I guess we'll leave you to it."

I followed my parents and Angus out the front door with my skates in hand and waited for them to reach their cars before I said, "Oh! My leg warmers!"

"It's not cold out," my mom said.

"It's a fashion choice," I said.

I went back through the house and past Bernadette, who was arranging flowers in a vase on the kitchen table.

Which was a problem.

Because from the kitchen, you could see the loft, where the beanbag chair was.

I hadn't factored in the presence of the realtor.

"You may want to check for dead flies in my parents' room," I said.

"Dead flies?" Bernadette studied me.

"Yeah, something died in the roof or something," I said. "The flies are getting into my parents' room and also dying. They don't even notice it anymore. Dustpan is in the laundry room. I'll show you."

Bernadette followed me to fetch the dustpan and hand broom. Then she headed for my parents' room and I bolted to my room, retrieved the cow pie, which smelled just as bad as it had yesterday, and returned to the loft and shoved it into the beanbag. It had the smell of chocolate chips to contend with but I figured that was a good thing. They'd think maybe the cookies were bad? Or that something had died behind the oven?

Bernadette was standing at the door of my parents' bedroom with a dustpan full of flies when I reached the hall with my leg warmers. "Thanks for the tip," she said.

"Any time!"

It felt weird to be leaving her there, alone at Big Red.

Out front, a car had already pulled into the driveway, where a FOR SALE sign with a yellow balloon had appeared, but I looked away. I didn't want to see who they were, what they were like. I knew I wouldn't be able to stand it if there was a girl like me, a girl luckier than me, who might inherit my house, my life.

My parents were both in my dad's car waiting for me. I got into the backseat. With Angus. I didn't understand why we weren't taking two cars. "Dad, are you coming roller-skating?"

It was my mother who answered. "Well, you're bringing a friend, so why shouldn't I?"

I snorted. "Dad's not your *friend*."

Dad said, "Of course I am." He looked out the window as we stopped at the end of the driveway and he reached over and squeezed her knee before pulling onto the road. "I'm her *best* friend." Then he smiled. "Remember that when I let you start dating when you're thirty."

"Fine by me," I said, thinking about Naveen. But maybe all of Stella's nagging about crushes was just getting to me. "I'm in no hurry."

"Atta girl," Dad said, and I smiled.

"What are we going to do with Angus?" I reached over and rubbed behind his ears. He looked half-asleep beside me.

"Dropping him off at Joe's for a few hours," my dad said.

We did that every once in a while, like if we were going to my grandparents' for a long visit. But today it felt especially sad to be sending poor Angus off to somebody else's house. When Angus climbed out of the car in front of Joe's and walked up onto his porch and laid down, I sort of wanted to go with him, and just wait out the open house, napping in the sun.

• • •

At the rink, Stella and I laced up as far away from my parents as we could.

"My dad would never go roller-skating," she said.

"First time for everything," I said.

"No, there isn't. Not for *my* dad. Your parents are just so *cool*."

I looked at them, trying to find cool things about them and failing. Why couldn't they get their act together and just be more grown-up and make more money and be more smart about things and not have to ruin everything?

"At least your dad has a job. That pays the bills," I said.

Stella fake-snored.

"Snore all you want." I stood on my skates, and nearly wiped out. "At least you can snore in your own bed in your own house and not have to shack up with your grandparents and then move who even knows where?"

She gave me a sad look and stood on her skates. "Come on." She grabbed my hand. "Let's skate it out."

It was hard to say no to someone wearing a purple satin one-piece jumpsuit who had blown her hair out in big feathery waves.

I was a bit wobbly at first since we hadn't skated in a few months, but I found my groove and got lost in the music and the lights reflecting off the disco ball that hung over the center of the oval rink. They sprayed across my dress like confetti and I felt just plain happy. Across the rink, on the opposite side, the light drizzled on my parents, who were skating side by side, lazily but somehow confidently, too. My dad reached out and took my mother's hand.

I wondered how my cow pie was doing and felt what might have been a twinge of regret.

Stella and I skated like crazy for forty-five minutes, then took a break on a bench near the lockers. Or at least I thought we were just taking a break, but Stella said, "My mom's actually picking me up in ten."

"What? Why?"

"I've been feeling bad about it since Thursday, but I can't keep it a secret either." Stella blew some hair out of her eyes. "I'm starting private classes with Miss Emma to prepare a solo for the competition."

"That's great," I said. "Why do you feel bad about it?"

"Because it's expensive and I know you probably can't, well, you know."

I hadn't even considered doing a solo.

Stella just nodded. "Yeah, my mom really wanted me to. And I really want to. I mean, dance is my passion. So she paid for a choreographer and now I need to meet with them and pick a song and I'll need extra sessions with Miss Emma."

"Wow." I felt, somehow, dumb. "I'm happy for you."

"Thanks." She hung her skates over her shoulder as she

stood, back in her normal shoes, looking short. "We'll talk later, okay?"

She went to the edge of the rink, waited for my mom to skate toward her, and said, "Thanks! My mom's here to pick me up!"

"Already?" My mom looked at me and back at Stella.

"Yeah, we've got a busy day!" Stella waved and took off, toward the arcade games near the exit, where my dad was shooting hoops.

Mom said, "Come skate with me."

So I did.

"I requested a few songs from *Xanadu*," she said, smiling a little. I had to work hard to smile back.

10.

Bernadette was sitting at the kitchen table when we got home after picking up Angus.

"Holy cow," my mom said, and I nearly laughed. "What's that smell?"

"A lot of folks were wondering the same thing." Bernadette's arms were crossed in front of her chest.

"Did someone track something in on their shoes?" Mom looked around at the floor.

"No," Bernadette said. "I opened some windows but it didn't really help. As you can tell, it's pretty pronounced. I explained that, of course, it was surely a one-time thing. It seemed to be originating here or up there." She pointed at the loft.

"We'll handle it before the next showing, whatever it is," Dad said.

At which point I realized I didn't have a plan for getting the fecal matter out of the beanbag and out of the house.

"Anyway, we had some pretty interested parties today." Bernadette collected her things. "I imagine at least one of them will want to come back and make sure the smell is gone. So we'll have another open house next weekend. After that we'll probably move to appointment only and see how we're doing."

"Okay," my dad said. "Thanks for everything. We'll get to the bottom of it for sure."

I *really* almost laughed.

When my parents were walking Bernadette to the door, I saw an opportunity. I ran upstairs, grabbed the beanbag, pulled out the bag of stink, and went to my room, where I figured I'd hang it out the window until I could get rid of it a better way. But out the window I saw Bernadette, getting into her car, which faced the house. If I opened the window and hung the bag out, she'd see me for sure. So I just waited.

"Kate!" my mom called out.

"Be right there!"

And waited.

"Come on, Bernie," I said softly.

I could hear my mother coming up the stairs.

The car still wasn't pulling out.

I thought the whole thing was going to end with me in major trouble for sure, but finally the car started moving.

Bernie's head went out of sight.

I opened the window and hooked the bag onto the hinge again.

Just in time.

"It even smells in here." I fanned the air in front of my face when my mother arrived at the doorway. "I just opened the window so hopefully that'll help."

"Yes," she said, sniffing. "It does seem to be fading, though, doesn't it? Anyway, why did Stella take off in such a hurry?"

Maybe this was my chance to explain about troupe. About how we couldn't move yet.

"Oh, she's doing private dance classes now," I said. "She's going to do that dance troupe thing and also compete as a soloist in the competition in June."

My mother sighed and sat on the bed and I thought maybe she'd ask me about troupe—what the details were, whether I wanted to do it, whether there was a way to make it work, whether I wanted to compete as a soloist, too, and how much it would cost.

She said, "I know you feel like you're the only one this is unfair for."

That's it? Really? That's all you've got? She was trying to tell me I shouldn't be sad and mad and *everything*—and she wasn't even doing it well!

She seemed done.

"You and Dad," I said. "You need to, you know, make more money than you do or something."

"Okay, Kate." She got up and drifted out of my room. "We'll do that. We'll go out and become millionaires any day now, just you wait."

I lay there for a while, looking out where the balloon on the FOR SALE sign bobbed in the wind. I reached out the window and threw the bag of turd into the front yard, then went downstairs and out the front door. I picked up the bag and walked around the back of the barn, where I hurled it into the woods. A few kittens I'd startled took a few leaps to another spot and settled again. "Sorry!" I said. They were already starting to get big.

I stopped at the FOR SALE sign on my way back up to the house, and untied the balloon. I let it go and watched as it went way high into the air, where it got so very tiny and then, finally, popped and disappeared in the sky's blue oblivion.

My stomach felt all twisty so I went inside to find my mom. She was lying on their bed, staring up at the way-high beams overhead. My parents' room, their walk-in closet, and their bathroom had walls that ended at normal height but no proper ceilings, just the peaked underside of the roof. All of which meant there wasn't a ton of privacy since it all just opened up to one big space and the stairs down to the living room. Even with the door to the bathroom closed, you could pretty much have a conversation with someone down in the kitchen.

When I was little, I'd wake up and climb into bed with my parents and we'd find owl faces and birds and deer with antlers in the knots in the wooden beams overhead. I climbed up onto the bed now and stared up at it with Mom, spotting some familiar shapes. The knot that looked like the man on the moon.

By the quarter-circle windows up near the ceiling, two flies were banging against the glass. "You think something is rotting up there?"

"Probably." My mother rolled over onto her side, curled up some, and pulled a throw over her legs.

"Are you going to try to find out?" I asked. The flies were pretty gross.

"Whatever it is will disappear eventually."

"What about the wasp's nest by my window?"

"Every time we have it taken down, they just build a new one."

It'd be nice to live in a house that had no nooks or crannies for wasps to make homes in or for rodents to die in. Maybe we'd downsize to a sleek apartment on the high floor of a building in some cute downtown area.

Then something out the floor-to-ceiling window at the end of the room caught my eye. I got up and spotted a flock of wild turkeys parading along the edge of the woods by the stream. They looked like visitors from another planet. I wanted to know if they knew their destination, and how they had all learned to stay together like that. Did any one of them ever just decide to up and move away to start anew? They disappeared down the stream toward the Nickersons' house.

I wondered if Pants had seen them, maybe hidden behind a tree.

I knew I was only delaying the inevitable.

I knew the day would come when the sale would happen.

I knew I wasn't going to miss the bees or dead flies—and I definitely wasn't going to miss the stinkbugs or Troy, who sometimes came home at midnight with the radio THAT LOUD—but I was going to miss the way living at Big Red was always at least a little bit interesting, and sometimes just plain beautiful.

I went into my room and pulled out the dance troupe permission slip and forged my mom's signature. Why should I be the only one who couldn't do it?

Down in the arts room, I made a diorama of my parents' room, drawing knotty shapes on wooden sticks on the ceiling and putting the three of us in bed—with me as a little kid, half their size—looking up in wonder.

11.

It was one of those weird things about us that Naveen and I barely talked on the bus. For whatever reason, seating was all boys with boys and girls with girls, and you mostly talked to who you sat with and no one thought to mess with that, not even me. I'd told Stella that the stink had been effective, but she didn't seem impressed so it wasn't until lunchtime that I got to enjoy my success.

"It worked!" I said to Naveen, as Stella wandered over to the lunch line. I held up a hand, which he high-fived, grabbed, and held for a second. His hand was warm, soft. "People were totally grossed out."

"Excellent," Naveen said. "So what's next?"

"There's another open house next weekend." My hand felt tingly from his.

"So you'll need more cow pie?" He rubbed his hands together.

It was cute how excited Naveen was, considering the topic.

"Or did you save it?" he asked.

"Yikes. I threw the bag into the woods." I hadn't actually thought to save it. Though I guessed that it would have been smart. I could probably find it again. Because the idea of going back to Depler's wasn't exactly thrilling.

"I don't know," I said. "Maybe I should mix it up. Do something different so Bernie doesn't catch on."

"Bernie?"

"The realtor's name is Bernadette but Bernie makes her seem like a less worthy foe."

Naveen laughed. "Kate: one. Bernie: zip."

"Exactly." I reached into my bag to find the list of things that smell. "What else was on that list of yours?"

I didn't even need to find the paper.

"Spoiled food," Naveen said. "Dead animals. Mildew. Cigarettes."

"The dead animal thing could work. If we could find one. Sometimes there are dead moles in the yard, but I don't know."

"It's not the *most* reliable plan," he said, "without the rodent in hand for a proper assessment of the stench potential."

Stench potential! Where did he even get this?

"There are flies coming into my parents' room. So it seems something dead is already around. Maybe I can find it?"

"Upstairs in the crazy room with no real walls?" Naveen furrowed his brow. "So the dead thing is probably in the roof?"

It wasn't ideal. Even if I were brave enough to *try* to get up there, there was the not-so-small issue of having to use a ladder and needing someone to hold the ladder.

"What's in your lunch box?" I asked Naveen as we reached our usual tables. "Anything that'll stink really bad in a few days?"

"Almond butter and jelly sandwich. Sorry."

I sat down at "my" table, which was next to the table Naveen shared with some of his guy friends. Stella appeared with her tray and sat down across from me, her earbuds in.

"I know!" I said to Naveen. "I'll raid the fridge this afternoon. For stuff that'll really stink by the end of the week. And I'll take it from there."

"Where are you going to put it to rot, though?" He bit his sandwich. Stella wasn't even listening.

I couldn't exactly keep it in my room. And outside there was the possibility of raccoons and wild animals having a feast. But then I remembered yet another forgotten project of my parents.

"The composting bin!" I said. "They stopped composting like two years ago."

"As previously discussed"—Naveen smiled—"you are shockingly good at this!"

"I know! It's like I've found my calling!"

Then Naveen started talking to his friends and I turned to Stella, who was humming along to her phone.

"Hello?" I said, waving a hand in front of her face. "Whatcha listening to?"

"Oh." She pulled out her earbuds and put them away. "I'm sorry. I'm out of it."

"What is it?"

"It's the song I'm dancing to. For my solo."

"Can I listen?"

"You sure?" She winced and made a sorry face.

"I'm sure, Stella. It's not like I even *want* to do a solo."

"Everybody wants to do a solo," she said.

I just looked at her for a second; she obviously had no idea what she sounded like. "I guess I'm not everybody."

She got her earbuds out again and I listened to the song. It was pretty, but it wasn't the best song I'd ever heard, and I felt glad about that for a second, then guilty.

"I like it," I concluded.

"Well, *I* love it," she said. "It's totally perfect for me."

I went back to studying my lunch. "What foods should I raid the fridge for that smell bad fast?"

Stella picked at her turkey sandwich. "I don't know, Kate. Are you sure this is a good idea?"

"I'm trying to make it to the end of the year. I'm trying to stay for Dance Nation. I thought you'd want that, too."

"Of course I do." She looked down at her fingernail. "But

you need the parent permission form signed."

"Don't worry your pretty head about it, Stella. I've got it all figured out."

I didn't, but I wanted her off my back.

Megan and her two sidekicks, Corinne and Natalie, walked up to our table. Megan said, "I saw a 'for sale' sign on your house."

"Yeah? So?" I took a bite of my sandwich, even though I was suddenly not very hungry.

"So where are you moving to?"

"Another house." I bugged out my eyes. "Duh."

"Where?"

"Not sure yet." Another bite. "We're looking around, trying to find just the right place."

Megan looked at her friends. "Pretty much anything you find is going to be nicer than that old place, right?"

"Yeah," I said. "Totally. We've seen some really awesome places already."

Megan and her friends walked off and I felt kind of pleased with how I'd handled that.

"Why did you do that?" Stella said.

"Because it's none of her business what's really going on."

"But she'll find out eventually."

"I'm not going to tell her. And you're not going to tell her. And Naveen doesn't speak to womenfolk other than us." At his table, he was laughing really hard about something, in a way that lit up his whole face.

Stella was flattening her aluminum foil. "Just so you know, I'm inviting her to my birthday party."

"Please tell me that's an April Fools' Day joke."

It was, in fact, April first.

June thirteenth still felt like a lifetime away, but I was one week closer.

"No joke." She wiped her mouth with her napkin and looked at me. "I mean, you're moving or *maybe* moving and I don't have a ton of friends. Anyway, there's a minimum at the karaoke place for kid parties."

"You're having a *karaoke* party?" This was bigger news than Megan being invited. "Oh, man, that's awesome. I always wanted a karaoke party."

"It's not my fault you haven't had one." Now she crumbled her tin foil into a ball.

"Uh," I said. "I never said it was."

"I know. I just, well . . . check this out." Stella dug around in her backpack and pulled out some small squares of paper. "It's the invitation I've been working on with my mom. And look, you'll get this slip of paper and you can preselect three songs."

The invitation was a picture of Stella seated at a piano and dressed up like a rock star with a lacy top and funky hair. Above her it said, GIRLS ROCK MAGAZINE'S GIRL OF THE YEAR TURNS 13. Then the party details ran down the side.

"This is going to be amazing!" I was picturing us doing totally over-the-top coordinated goofball dance moves. I studied the date. "Two weeks!"

"And . . . ," Stella said, taking the invitation back. "I'm inviting boys!"

And then my whole fantasy went poof.

"Noooooo," I said. *"Why?"*

"Because it'll be fun. Because I *like* boys."

For whatever reason—probably the same reason the bus seating was the way it was—people had pretty much stopped having boy/girl parties when we were maybe six. So for years birthdays had involved just us girls at the spa in town, or roller-skating, or pumpkin-picking. I liked it that way. It was easy. No pressure. Karaoke with boys sounded very much like something other people did. Older people.

I read through the guest list she held out to me and saw Naveen's name.

"Maybe Naveen will do a duet with me," I said. "For kicks."

Stella shook her head. "People are going to start thinking you like him."

"Of course I like him."

"No, I mean, *like* him like him."

"Don't be ridiculous." I didn't mention how my hand still sort of tingled. I studied the other boys on her list. "Tris Culpberg, really?"

"Why not?"

"Because I've never even seen you say two words to him."

"How do you know?" Stella gathered her stuff to get up. "We're not joined at the hip."

"Fine. Invite anybody you want."

"I will," she said. "I'm inviting Sam Fitch. For you."

"For me?"

"For you."

"Don't do me any favors," I said.

Ugh!

I knew that it was going to happen eventually—crushes, dates, hand-holding, slow dancing, kissing. I just didn't know *how*. And while it was true that I liked how Sam looked and felt a little funny when he talked to me, I wasn't sure if that was what a crush felt like. And since I didn't much like the feeling, I had sort of been hoping not.

"You're coming to my house after dance today, right?" she asked.

"Yeah." My parents both had actual work to do until dinnertime, so that was the plan.

"Great, so we can think about what to wear." She put her earbuds in and left the table.

12.

When we were on our way into the dance studio after school, Stella said, "Don't mention my party, okay? I'm not inviting everyone from class."

I hadn't thought about her party in hours.

We got changed fast and lined up by the door to the studio as the tiny dancers paraded out. My troupe forms shook slightly in my hands because my whole body was vibrating with excitement.

"How are my dancers?" Miss Emma asked as we all walked into the studio.

Everyone muttered good's and hi's and she said, "I see a lot of troupe forms. Excellent!"

She started going around collecting papers, making sure everything was properly filled out. My heartbeat quickened when she was reviewing my parent form, but she seemed totally happy. I made a point of not looking at Stella.

Miss Emma collected the last form and said, "I'm so excited! You're all on board. So let's get to work." She turned on our song. "Just dance however you want to limber up."

The second time through, she gave us all our opening positions. "You're all advanced enough that we're going to try to run through the whole thing today. Then we'll add blocking Thursday. Ready?"

We all said, "Ready!"

And the hour was a blur of leaps and kicks and slides and more. One thing I liked about contemporary dancing was that there weren't names for everything the way there was with ballet. It felt like the most freeing kind of dancing to me. We learned mostly from watching Miss Emma and imitating her. It was something I was good at.

We were all sweating when she said, "Okay, from the top. One last time. Let's see how you do."

She cued up the song again and I imagined us all on a stage together.

Big lights.

A full auditorium.

The hairs on my arms perked up.

I'd already committed most of the routine to memory.

The music kicked in and we went for it and even though we all made a few mistakes, it was pretty great for a first practice. Miss Emma clapped when we were done and we clapped, too. I

was dying of thirst so I headed for the water fountain.

"Don't you think you should maybe tell Miss Emma?" Stella asked, after I drank. "That you might not even be living here in June?"

"I've already got the situation under control." I wiped water from my lips with my arm.

"You can't actually be serious."

"It only has to work for a few weeks, and anyway, my dad said if they ended up selling really close to the end of school year we could talk about me staying with you. End of the school year puts me in range of Dance Nation. No problemo."

"I hope you're right," Stella said. "Because it'd be really unfair for us all to learn the routine one way if we're going to have to change it at the last minute."

"I'm sorry if my misery is inconvenient for you."

She huffed.

We went and packed up our stuff.

Miss Emma stopped me on the way out and pulled me aside. "I was hoping you'd consider doing a solo, Kate."

"Oh." I was sort of shocked that she was saying this. "I'm more of a team player, I think?"

"I happen to think you could do a really great job and that it might be good for you to step into the spotlight and not hide in the group."

I'd never thought about it that way. "I'm not hiding," I said.

Miss Emma squeezed my arm gently. "Just think about it."

13.

When Stella and I were younger, our favorite thing to do had been playing with Stella's Barbie styling head doll. We'd given that poor, long-gone Barbie about a million makeovers. But now when I came over, we mostly just hung out and listened to music and watched dance competition videos and talked. Sometimes we did our homework because it was more fun doing it together than alone.

"We need to figure out what to wear for my party!" Stella went to her closet.

I flopped down onto her bed and groaned, but at least she wasn't bugging me about dance troupe.

What would doing a solo even feel like?

"Here." Stella tossed a dress at me. "Try this on."

"I'm sorry," I said. "You must have mistaken me for someone else."

I think I might have gotten it from my mother, who was always in leggings and big sweaters or oversize shirts, but I just wasn't that into fashion. I did love the way that dance costumes—with their shiny fabrics and sequins and fringes—seemed to transform me into someone else entirely, but in the day to day, I just didn't care that much.

"Just try it," Stella said. "You might like it."

As Stella changed out of her school clothes into a blue dress that shimmered, I slid into the dress she'd handed me. It was floral and girlie and not at all my kind of thing. I turned to her and frowned.

"Fine, forget it."

I changed back into my clothes and felt normal again. So normal that I dared to bring up dance class. "Miss Emma told me she thought I should do a solo."

Stella froze for a second. "Really?"

"Yeah. Why do you seem surprised?"

"I don't know. It just doesn't seem like dance is your passion or anything."

"Are worms eating your brain or something? You're saying the weirdest stuff all of a sudden."

"What?" She shrugged. "I'm just saying you don't seem to love it."

"Well, I do." Now I shrugged. "I just think dancing is more

fun with other people than alone."

"Then tell her that." She turned to the mirror to look at herself. "I wouldn't want us to be competing against each other anyway."

"Why not?"

"Because what if one of us won or something? The other one would have her feelings hurt." She was brushing her hair.

"You mean me," I said, slowly. "*I* would have my feelings hurt."

She put the brush down and put her hands on her hips. "How did we get into this thing?"

"I have no idea."

"My point really is that your parents would never spend that money if you might not be here to see it through."

"No, of course not," I said.

It was true.

Then I heard the doorbell. My mother was here to pick me up. I didn't normally but today I leapt up to gather my things.

"Hey, what's all this stuff?" I asked, peeking inside a bag by the bed where a bunch of Barbies swam in weird positions in a pool of clothes.

"I'm too old for Barbies." Stella was trying on yet another dress. "I don't even know why they're still around."

"Kate!" my mom called.

"I guess I'll see you tomorrow," I said, and I grabbed my backpack. Looking at the bag of Barbies, I noticed the fabric of one of the dresses. "Can I take them? The Barbies?"

"*You're* too old for Barbies," Stella said.

"I want the clothes for a project." I didn't feel like explaining about the dioramas I'd been making, but when I looked at those tiny dresses, I saw fabrics perfect for curtains and bedspreads and more.

"Knock yourself out," Stella said.

"I'm just going to the bathroom," I called out once I was in the hall, and my mom said, "Okay!"

I went into the bathroom and closed the door. I sat on the toilet and realized I could hear my mom's voice.

"Honestly," she said. "I have a lot of anger. I'm not sure what to do about it. It's not like I'm not also responsible. It's not rational. But I'm angry." I held my breath and waited, holding in pee. "At *him*."

It took me a minute to figure out that she was talking about my dad.

Was divorce still a possibility?

"Don't take this the wrong way, Liv," Stella's mom said. "But it sounds like you may be depressed."

"Of course I'm depressed." My mom laughed, but it wasn't a happy laugh. "I'm losing my house."

"I mean, *clinically*." Stella's mom lowered her voice but she was typically pretty loud so I could still hear her. "It might be good to talk to someone."

"He said the same thing, but I'm talking to *you*." My mother laughed stiffly. "Isn't that enough?

"I don't know, Liv. I honestly don't."

I flushed and walked out into the hall.

• • •

When we got home, the stereo was blasting another one of Dad's band's songs. A ballad called "Super Powers" that always cracked me up because it's about a guy who has powers like having fun when he's alone and knowing how to get off the phone. Now it seemed a little sad to me, my dad having written a song about a lame superhero.

The whole house seemed to shake as my dad sang, *"Look at me. I've got super powers."*

He had the windows open and we could see him, down by the patio near the tennis court, dancing slowly while he swept up debris that had fallen from the trees. Angus was lying near an Adirondack chair.

Years ago, my parents had a party where they'd strung all these lanterns from the weeping willow. I was running around all weekend with my cousins, and friends were coming and going, and we were launching these glowing rocket things into the air at dark.

I was about to ask my mother if she remembered that weekend, that party, but then she turned down the music. "I'm going to go lie down. Can you go tell Dad we're home and to get dinner started?"

"Sure," I said.

She left the room and I watched out the window as my dad just kept on dancing for a few minutes, finishing the song exactly in time with the music playing softly in the house. Then he turned and saw me standing there. I waved and he waved for me to come down. So I did.

When I got down to the yard, he was sitting in a patio chair, smoking a cigarette. "Don't tell your mother," he said.

"That you're the world's worst dancer?" I snorted. The cigarette made my dad look like an entirely different person. "Pretty sure she already knows."

"It's just one. I'm not going to start smoking or anything."

"Okay, Dad." I knew he had smoked a bit when they were in the band, and I sometimes smelled cigarettes on nights when my parents were hanging out past my bedtime outside with friends, but I'd never actually seen him do it myself. It made him look younger somehow. But also shaky? Stressed?

"How was school?" he asked, exhaling, laying his head back on the chair and looking up at the weeping willow.

"It was school." We just sat there quietly for a while. A thick white cloud drifted out from behind the willow like a slow-moving cruise ship, and I realized I'd just missed a great opportunity to grab some food for the rotting project.

"Do you remember that party?" I said, after a while. "With the movie projected on the sheet? And all those lanterns in the tree?"

"Barely," he said, and he laughed. "I mean, of course I do. Why?"

I shrugged. "Are things going to be like that again, do you think?"

Pants and two kittens appeared across the yard by the pear tree. Angus lifted his head and put it down again.

"Depends on what you mean by 'like that'?"

"I don't know." My throat tightened. "Happy?"

"Of course they are, Kate." He shook his head and looked up toward Big Red. "It's just a house."

But he didn't sound convinced.

I sat back in my chair and watched the wind blow the weeping willow's long soft branches. I loved that tree. Loved how when it was in full bloom some of its branches brushed the grass, how you could hide behind strands of leaves during a game of hide-and-seek. A tree expert who my parents had hired to take down some dead trees a few years back had studied this one, with a huge hollow dead branch broken off the main trunk, just hanging there. He told us that, sure, he could cut it off but it would just happen again. The tree was fine. That's just what weeping willows did. They let part of themselves die so the rest could live.

I thought about asking my dad if my mom was depressed. But he looked pretty down himself, and I wasn't sure there was much point. So I got up and grabbed my scooter from the shed and started making lazy circles on the tennis court. After a few jumps and tricks, I said, "Oh, Mom said to tell you to get dinner started."

He took a final drag of his cigarette and stubbed it out on the bottom of his shoe then got out his phone. Holding it to his ear as I balanced on one foot with a long leg out behind me like an ice skater, he asked, "Pepperoni or plain?"

• • •

After pizza and homework, I went downstairs and started to play around with some green yarn and tiny bits of green paper. When I had the hang of making tree branches, I searched around but there were no more shoeboxes down there, so I went up to ask my mom if I could raid her closet. My parents were sitting in the living room, each of them reading in an armchair. When they were like this, so normal, so boring looking, it was hard to imagine when they met and were younger and, well, cooler.

"Mom, can I grab a shoebox from your closet?"

"Sure," she said.

So I did that, but on my way back downstairs, I said, "I'm going to have ice cream. Anybody want any?"

"No, thanks," they both said. I went to the kitchen and got out a Tupperware and took two eggs and a piece of chicken out of the refrigerator. I cut open the plastic on the chicken and slid it into the Tupperware, then quietly cracked the eggs on top of it and closed it up. I figured it wouldn't stink for a while so I just stashed it way in the back of the pantry for safekeeping. I fixed a bowl of ice cream, grabbed the bag of Barbies I'd left by the front door, and went back downstairs.

As soon as I started making the weeping willow for real, I got the idea to turn the box on its side so that it was more tall than wide. I lined the walls of the box with black construction paper, then cut a strip of a sort of gray/brown felt into the shape of a tree trunk and glued it to the back wall. Then, one by one, I took my strips of green yarn, each of which I'd tied still more yarn to, and so on and so on, to create the look of the weeping branches, gluing them to the top of the box so they draped down. It took a while, but it was shaping up to really look like a tree so I kept at it. When it was done, I took some of these little furry glitter balls I had hanging around in a jar and threaded string into them with a needle. I made five of them in different colors before I started hanging them from the tree.

Party lights.

From the bag of Barbies, I pulled out a dress made of red gingham fabric and cut out the largest square I could get out of it.

A blanket for stargazing.

When I decided to take a break for ice cream before putting myself and maybe some cousins in the scene, I saw that it had melted.

I went ahead and finished the scene.

• ● •

In the living room my dad was asleep on the couch.

Upstairs, my mother was reading in bed.

When I poked my head in to say good night to her, Angus got up and followed me into my room.

14.

I had zero opportunity to retrieve my Tupperware of Stink from the pantry Tuesday morning but it
seemed unlikely anyone would find it before I got home.
My mom had a day of networking for a bunch of Hudson
Valley lawyers to oversee; my dad was designing a book
cover on a rush schedule and also announced that he
was working on a new song. He'd be headphoned and
out of it all day. For the first time in forever, it seemed
like maybe they were actually making some money, but
it was too late.

"Oh," Stella said, when we got off the bus. "Here."

She took a tall stack of envelopes out of her backpack
and handed me the top one.

"Oh," I said. "Cool."

· I hadn't been sure whether we'd had a fight or not, so I was a little bit relieved.

Then Stella was off flitting around, handing out invitations here and there and by lunchtime, all any of our friends were talking about was Stella's party. I sort of felt bad for people who weren't invited, maybe because I knew what that felt like. But I slapped on a smile and joined the conversation Stella was having with our friends Sara and Maggie.

"I want to sing this one," Sara pointed at a list of songs they'd been studying.

"Oh, sorry," Stella said. "Birthday girl calls dibs on that one."

Maggie said, "I want number seven-eight-six-four. Write that down for me!"

"Oh," Stella said. "Really? I have that on my list, too."

The boy thing was bad enough, but with Stella going all diva, it really didn't seem like this party was going to be any fun at all.

"You'll have to take a break for cake at some point, eh, Stella?" I said.

Maggie smiled. Sara laughed.

"Ha ha," Stella said. "Very funny."

Then the bell rang and we had to hurry to Gym, where we were playing kickball, a game that I found to be fun for the three seconds it took to kick. Otherwise it seemed there was a lot of waiting around. Unless you got picked to "pitch" like Sam Fitch did, mostly because he was better than any-body else at actually getting the ball to roll over the plate.

At one point, at least, I ended up waiting in line to kick with Naveen next to me.

"So." He seemed amused. "You going to the big party?" He waved his hands like he was a crazy person.

"Right? It's not just me?"

He nodded a few times, slowly. "She's excited, that's for sure."

"I'm her best friend, so I'll be there. You?"

"Totally." He nodded then flashed his sly smile; one of his front teeth was just slightly crooked. "I bet you don't know this about me, but I'm a pretty good singer."

"You're pretty good at everything, Naveen."

"I take offense to that!" He nudged me. "I *excel* at most things. I'm *pretty good* at a few additional things."

"What are you going to sing?"

"I haven't decided yet. I'm going to spend some time considering the options. They have them on the website."

"Cool." I hadn't managed to even peek at the list the girls had at lunch so I had no idea what I would sing.

"How about you?"

"I don't know." I really didn't understand the whole plan-ning ahead thing. "Maybe some eighties hair metal. My dad's way into that stuff so I know a ton of lyrics."

"That'd be awesome." Naveen nodded.

"Right?!"

We both laughed.

"Did you get your food stewing?"

"I did."

"Awesome."

But then Naveen looked sort of faraway and sad, and I said, "What?"

"You *know* you won't be able to keep it up forever."

"I know." It felt like a bubble popping between us.

"It's pretty sad to think somebody might knock Big Red down," he said.

"What are you even talking about?"

"I looked it up. The listing for the house. The ad said it was a fixer-upper or possible partial teardown on amazing property."

I felt sick. "A teardown?"

"They said something like 'possible reno to suit your vision' but that means teardown." He took my elbow and we both moved forward in the line. "Sorry, Kate. I figured you knew."

It was my turn to kick. I fouled out twice and then, on my third kick, I nailed it. But it flew right at Sam Fitch, and he caught it. Pop fly out.

"Sorry, Kate!" he called out as I walked back to the end of the line.

"Not your fault!" I said, feeling my palms start to sweat.

What was that even about?

• ● •

At home that afternoon, when I saw my parents were both distracted by their own tasks, I got my Tupperware out of the pantry and walked down to where the old composting bin had ended up, overgrown behind the garden. I opened the lid, placed the container inside, and closed the bin.

With any luck it would reek by Saturday.

Then I went up to the computer and found realtor.com and looked up my address. The listing loaded, with photo after photo of my house. I clicked on the picture of my own room, the ballerina print still on the wall, the paisley of the bedspread looking lovely. When had they even taken that picture? It felt weird how much they'd done behind my back.

I opened the pop-up slideshow so that I could study the pictures more closely. Everything looked funny. Like my parents had hurriedly cleared off surfaces and moved chairs to get better shots. Probably Bernie had come to help. Probably when I was at school.

I exhaled so hard that my hair moved.

The picture of the old bathroom with the claw-foot tub was especially lovely. Then there were pictures of the stream, the garden, and the barn. I tried to imagine what I'd think if I were someone shopping for a house, but it was impossible for me to separate out what I knew.

I scrolled back up and read the description:

> Just minutes from the Shawangunk Mountains and surrounded by apple orchards is this 1900 farmhouse on a country road. A 1998 post and beam addition, including a stone fireplace, brings charm, warmth, and style together all in one sweet home, and is in great shape. Older farmhouse section needs TLC or possible reno to suit your vision. Outbuilding has great guesthouse potential. Original wide board floors, beamed ceilings, eat-in kitchen, and two staircases. Enjoy the private backyard from the walk-out lower level with a small seasonal stream and grape arbor. A rocking chair front porch is just one of the special characteristics still evident from yesteryear.

I actually said, "Oh, give me a break," out loud.

Because: "Yesteryear"?

Was that even a word?

TLC, I could totally see. Especially since my parents had sort of let things go recently. But the idea that someone might tear down the old section seemed crazy.

Then I saw another note that made my skin feel tight. "Great potential as a second home for city dwellers. Only 90 minutes from the heart of NYC!"

So someone could buy our house, our *home*, and then *not even live in it*.

I looked at the price: $285,000.

That was a lot of money. But it wasn't a ton of money, like a million. Still, we should be able to buy a house with that. Another smaller house, right? Why weren't we doing that? I clicked around and found a few cute-looking, two-bedroom houses for half the money. Why did we have to move in with my grandparents at all?

I went into the old bathroom and started to fill the claw-foot tub. It was the middle of the day, but I didn't care. Then I added some bubble bath to really make it worth my while—also to hide the blue lime stains near the drain—and got in, careful to close the doors so that they actually stayed shut.

The wall I was facing was covered in old-fashioned patterned blue wallpaper that had roosters and tall grasses in its design. There was a long-standing joke between my father and his friends about him liking roosters. Like someone spread the word that he liked roosters as a joke and it stuck? Hanging there on the wall were a bunch of framed cut-paper silhouettes. One of me, one of my mom, one of my dad—all of them made at some colonial village we'd visited when I was about seven—then two of my grandparents. They looked good there, old-fashioned. I hated to think they wouldn't always be there, that the new owners would probably tear down the rooster paper at the first opportunity. That the old tub, which had lasted THIS LONG, might end up in a landfill somewhere. Or worse, taken outside and converted into a flowerbed.

I sunk down so my ears were underwater and swished water around with my hands.

"Kate?" My mother's voice penetrated the water. "You in there?"

I said, "Yup!" and sat up a bit.

"Are you *in the bath*?"

"Yup!"

"Kate." She poked her head in. "You're going to be dirtier now than you were before. Did you clean it first?"

I sunk back down. "Nope." There were probably some dusty bits floating around, but the bubbles hid them pretty well.

She sighed and shook her head and closed the door.

• • •

Mom was unwrapping trays of food in the kitchen, rearranging, putting some in Tupperware, when I paraded through with just my towel on.

"What's all this?" I asked.

She was at the Tupperware drawer, looking around.

"Leftovers from a conference," she said, still looking. "Where's that good square Tupperware with the red lid?"

"Sorry, Mom." I pictured my food festering in it out back. "I don't really keep track of the Tupperware."

"I can't find the spatula either. Do you think someone *stole* them? Like at the open house?"

"That would be pretty weird. Better get Bernie on the case."

"Anyway," she said. "Everything was delicious, we just

had too much of it. Should get us through the week."

"Leftovers all week," I said. "Yay."

I got dressed in comfy clothes and was going to do homework in my room but then I heard my mother on the phone talking to my aunt Michelle, best I could tell, and it sounded like she was crying. I heard sniffling, and "I know, I know," and "yeah, maybe," and "but you know me, I don't even like to take Advil."

It was hard to be angry after that.

When she hung up, I went back downstairs to do homework at the dining room table. My mom was there, on her computer, probably just emailing. I wanted to be in the same room with her.

"Mom?" I said after a while.

"Yeah?"

"It's a lot of money, right? Two hundred and eighty-five thousand?"

"How did—?"

"It's called the Internet."

"Of course," she said.

"Won't that sort of make us rich? Like we could buy a house that cost a little less than that and still have money left over."

"It's a bit more complicated than that, honey. And you really shouldn't be worrying or thinking about any of this."

"So I'm supposed to pretend it isn't happening?"

She sighed. "We paid more for the house than we're trying to sell it for is the long and short of it. The market bottomed out and we hit the bottom, too. And we borrowed against the house at one point. So we need to sell and pay down some debt and then start over."

I didn't entirely understand how mortgages worked. But it didn't sound good.

"So we won't actually have any of that money to spend."

She shook her head.

"How did that even happen?" I asked.

She got up and said, "I need to lie down."

I followed her a few minutes later, and climbed onto her bed. I wanted to apologize, but I also wanted *her* to apologize. I wanted everything to be different, to be like it used to be.

"There." I pointed at some knots in the wood beams overhead. "An owl in flight." I looked around some. "And there, a deer head."

My mom sniffled a bit beside me.

"Over there," I said. "An upside-down dog."

Then she started crying really hard.

"It'll be okay, Mom." I swallowed hard. "I'm sorry I brought it up."

She bit her bottom lip and nodded.

15.

My mother mentioned over breakfast that Bernie was getting a ton of calls and wanted to have two open houses this weekend instead of one. If Bernie was escalating things, I had to also. I asked Naveen if he could come over to consult on where best to put the rotting food and he said yes.

My mother was working that afternoon, so I texted my dad to ask if Naveen could come over to study and he said, **Sure thing.**

I coasted through the school day, just counting the hours until it was done.

There was a chalkboard over the kitchen sink where my parents and I left notes for each other. When I got home, I saw my dad had written, *Running a few errands. Back in twenty.*

Which was typical of my dad. There seriously weren't any errands you could run around our house that would take only twenty minutes. It took ten minutes to get any-where. Also, he hadn't written down the time he left. Had it already been twenty minutes ago?

It didn't matter.

I knocked off a few pages of homework with Angus lying by my feet, and then I heard the sound of bike wheels crunching on gravel and went to the front door.

I'd just gotten off the bus with Naveen a few minutes ago, but he'd changed clothes and looked like a completely different person. In school, Naveen had the "star student" look—white shirt tucked into khaki pants—but after school he was more of a goof. Today he was wearing orange jeans and a shirt with a Wookiee on it. I liked both versions of him.

"We lucked out," I said. "My parents aren't even home. My dad could be back any minute now, but hopefully we can figure this out fast."

"I'm ready," Naveen said. "Give me the tour."

"You know Big Red."

"Ah, but I don't *know* Big Red. I mean, like, secret passage-ways, old staircases. Anything like that? We usually hang out outside."

"Hmmm," I said. "Sort of."

I took Naveen downstairs—Angus followed—and showed him the closet under the stairs, the room where my dad kept his tools, the old staircase to nowhere in the craft room, and finally, the bar. "This is the tail end of the tour, right?" he asked. "So people are probably not spending most of their time here."

"Good point."

We went back upstairs to the main floor, where I showed him the laundry room, which had a bunch of exposed pipes for a ceiling, and I took him upstairs to my parents' bedroom, where I explained again about the flies—ten more dead ones on the floor.

Naveen took a minute to walk around.

"This house is so weird," he said.

"I know. That's why I love it."

He poked his head into the bathroom. "What if you put it way up on that top shelf?" There was a tall rack for towels and toiletries in canvas bins way high behind the door.

My parents always told this story, about the time I'd had a friend over for a playdate when I was maybe six. At that point, I was sleeping in bunk beds that the previous owners had left behind in the room adjoining my parents' room that was now the walk-in closet. My preschool friend, Kayla, had somehow found the car key and had been playing on the top bunk. She left it up there, on top of the wall of the room. My parents had looked for the car key for hours before they thought to send me up to the bunk bed to look on that ledge.

I told Naveen the short version. "I'll use smaller pieces of the food in smaller bags and put them on top of the walls of all the rooms without ceilings." I turned around in the hall-way, looking at all the air up there. "It will make this whole floor reek!"

"That sounds like an excellent plan." We high-fived.

We went down to the kitchen and made a snack—melting cheddar cheese onto tortilla chips—then talked through the logistics of how I'd store and plant the stink.

"What's with all the dioramas?" he asked when we were done.

It took me a minute to realize what he was talking about, that he'd have seen them all downstairs.

"I don't know. Just something I'm doing. It's making me kind of sad, actually. But somehow making me feel better, too."

"Can we go look at them?" He ate another chip, one with a ton of cheese on it.

So we went back downstairs and I showed him the diorama of the clubhouse, and the weeping willow, and my parents' room, and my room. I lined them all up alongside each other. I hadn't actually realized how many there were.

"Kate," Naveen said. "These are amazing."

"Thanks. I want to do the old bathroom next. I'm just trying to figure out the best way to make a miniature claw-foot tub."

Maybe I could use one of the boats I'd made out of milk cartons and straws at a school craft fair a while back?

I climbed up on a chair and dug around through some crates and found them. They didn't look quite right for my diorama but they appeared to be possibly still seaworthy.

"Want to race boats in the stream?" I asked Naveen.

"Absolutely."

There were some bees flying around the top of the back porch stairs but I took a deep breath and walked quickly past them and down to the stream. We walked along it toward the tennis court and went out onto the boards that formed the bridge into the woods. Kneeling down beside each other, Naveen and I each took a boat and held it just above the water. It was running slow and steady. Perfect for racing.

"On your mark," I said. "Get set." We smiled. "Go."

We put our boats in the water and got up to walk alongside them as they were carried down the current.

"Go, go, go!" Naveen screamed.

"Easy does it," I said, as my boat went over a rock but managed to remain upright.

They were neck and neck for a while, but then Naveen's boat got caught on a branch and mine hit the small waterfall near the pear tree too fast and capsized. Naveen's broke free from the branch and he called out, "Here she comes!"

He stood beside me as we watched his boat weather the waterfall perfectly.

"Woohoo!" I said. "She made it!"

"Doesn't that mean you lost?" Naveen laughed.

"So?"

"I swear, Kate. You're like the least competitive I person I know."

"Is that a bad thing?" I was feeling a lot of competition with Stella lately. But it was mostly in my head. Or was it in hers?

"No," he said. "It's just . . . unusual."

I retrieved my boat with the help of a nearby stick, and Naveen and I walked downstream to see where his boat had ended up. After we found it, we sat on the bench under the pear tree.

"I'm going to miss you," Naveen said. "*If* you end up leaving, I mean."

I couldn't speak.

We both knew it would happen eventually.

"I'm going to miss hanging around Big Red, too," he said. "But mostly you."

"Aw, thanks, Naveen." My heart felt strange, like someone had just grabbed it with a fist. "I think maybe I don't like change very much."

"Nobody does." He flicked a bug off his leg.

The wind blew and some leaves skipped across the grass in front of us. "Do you think maybe it's because I've never really had any?"

"I haven't either." He flicked another bug. "Not really."

I elbowed him. "What'd those bugs ever do to you?"

I heard the sliding door open and turned toward the house.

"I'm home!" My dad looked so small up there on the back porch. "Hi, Naveen!"

"Hi, Mr. Marino!" Naveen waved.

When my dad waved back he accidently hit my mother's wind chimes and they sang, loudly. My dad covered his ears and laughed.

• • •

At dinner, we talked about how we were going to spend the open houses, 12–2 both days. On Saturday, Mom wanted to go horseback riding. Dad wanted to find someplace to take archery lessons. On Sunday the plan was to go see my grandparents.

"Why can't we just go to a movie? Maybe a Chinese buffet? Or both?" I asked.

"Because we're trying to broaden our horizons," my mother said.

"We are?" I asked.

"We are." She was making plates of leftovers. Chicken and rice. Some kind of brown beef dish. I guessed it was good she wasn't going to miss the chicken I'd taken, or the eggs.

"Anyway," she said. "We'll do some research, figure it out. Maybe we can do both."

"Isn't that stuff expensive?" If they weren't going to think about this stuff, *someone* had to.

My mom froze and looked at my dad. He said, "Like your mom said, we'll do some research."

"In the meantime," my mother said. "You've made quite a mess downstairs. There are tiny pieces of paper and fluff everywhere. You need to tidy up all that craft stuff before Saturday."

After dinner, when tasked with taking the trash out, I went down into the woods to check on the progress of my Tupperware of Stink. I opened the composting bin and didn't smell much, so I reached for the container and unsnapped the red lid. I sniffed the air then regretted it. Imagine a zombie chicken that threw up a milk shake.

I closed the lid again and put the container back in the composting bin and turned to head inside when I heard a meowing sound. I tried to locate it and saw one of Pants's kittens stuck on the other side of the stream.

"It's okay, cutie." I went to the nearest footbridge and bent down. "Come on over."

It took her a while but she came to me and I lifted her back over to Big Red.

16.

"You're up early," I said, when I came into the kitchen to find my dad pouring himself a cup of coffee Thursday morning.

"You, my dear"—he yawned—"are quite mistaken."

He looked pretty ragged.

"You never went to bed?"

"Ding, ding, ding." He used a finger to tap the air three times.

"Why? What happened?"

"This song I'm working on. I can't get it out of my head. I needed to get some stuff down."

"What kind of song is it?" I asked.

If my dad was suddenly going to start trying to play in a rock band again, I thought now might be a good time to crawl up into a ball and hide in a faraway corner of some faraway barn.

"Just music, really. I don't know. I'm going to send it on to Shay. See if he can find a home for it."

"That sounds exciting." I poured myself some cereal.

"Want to sit outside with me for a few?"

"I would, but the bees always go for my cereal."

"Suit yourself." He opened the door to the back porch, put his sunglasses on, and stepped out.

I sat at the kitchen table and looked out the window at him. We used to pretend sometimes that that window between the kitchen and the porch was for a short order cook or fast-food drive-in.

There was a stinkbug on the window, trying to get out and failing miserably. Their numbers seemed to be dropping off, at least. I couldn't remember the last time I'd seen one.

I finished my breakfast, said bye to my dad, and headed out. On the bus, Stella asked for my party RSVP.

I snorted. "I already told you I'm coming."

The party was a little over a week away so I needed to start thinking of a present to get her.

"I know, but I need the form back," Stella said. "With your song choices."

"Can't I just decide that day? It's not like I'm going to practice."

"You're not?"

I shook my head. "It's karaoke, Stella. It's not like I'm going to get discovered."

"You might! Like by, you know, a *boy*."

I laughed. "Let it go, Stella!"

"I just think you could put a little effort in."

"All right, Stella. I'll fill out the form tonight. Scout's honor."

Megan was waiting just outside the bus for Stella when we got off. She held out an envelope and said, "I may have to leave early, but I'm coming."

"Great!" Stella said. "Did you pick songs?"

"I did. I don't know why I never thought of having a karaoke party but it's an awesome idea."

"Thanks," Stella said.

"I actually don't remember going to *any* of your birthday parties, Megan," I said. I turned to Stella. "Do you, Stella?"

"No," Stella said. "But whatever. Thanks for RSVP'ing, Megan."

· ● ·

At dance class that afternoon, we went right back to learning the routine and I liked how it all was coming together so fast. What I didn't like was how Stella kept drifting off to a corner during breaks and doing *other* steps while staring at herself in the mirror. I imagined they were from her solo and I had to admit I was sort of mad about it.

"You're distracting everybody," I said at one point.

"I am not," she said.

"Fine. Whatever."

I wasn't lying. I was so distracted by the fact that she

was working on her solo during troupe that I kept missing steps and once I even bumped right into Madison.

"Am I the only one who sees what she's doing?" I asked Madison, who shrugged and said, "It's annoying but whatever."

During a quick water break, Miss Emma said, "I'm hearing a lot of side chatter, ladies. What's going on?"

I said, "Stella's distracting everyone by sneaking off to practice her solo."

Stella huffed. "Kate might be moving. And I thought you should know. So you don't have to redo the whole troupe routine if it happens."

Miss Emma looked at me, her eyes losing some of their sheen. Then she turned to the group and said, "Take it from the top. Excuse us for a minute."

She ushered me into the changing room. "Kate? Is it true?"

And there was something in her tone of voice, something in the sad concern in her eyes that just got to me.

I burst into tears.

"Oh my gosh, I'm so sorry. I didn't mean to." She pulled me into a hug with her long, slender arms. "It'll be okay. Tell me what's going on."

"They put the house up for sale, it's true. I mean, who knows how long it'll take but yeah. I don't even know if I'll be here three weeks from now let alone in the lead-up to the competition."

"But they let you sign up, right?"

I nodded.

I was a horrible person.

"This is what we're going to do." Miss Emma pulled out of the hug and held me by the shoulders. "Let's just keep on keeping on with the rehearsals, and we'll see what happens. Sometimes these things take a while. They wouldn't have let you sign up otherwise! But you really do have to promise to keep me updated. What do you say? Stay focused? Hope for the best?"

It sounded so simple.

Hope for the best!

"Okay." I nodded.

We went back to dancing. The song was just hitting the second chorus so I fell into line and nailed a knee-spin move like I'd never nailed it before.

•••

Stella and I didn't speak to each other—only to my mother—on the way home, but I don't think my mom even noticed.

At home I went straight down to the arts room and gathered up the Barbie dolls and threw them out. I hadn't even wanted the dolls—only the clothes—so it was sort of a pointless gesture but somehow it felt good anyway.

There was a text from Stella on my phone.

Are you mad at me?

I lay there on my bed for a while, thinking about how much *my life* stank and how awesome Stella's life was.

Solo!

Karaoke thirteenth birthday!

Horse camp!

She had to *ask*?

It felt good, in a way, that Miss Emma knew. But I didn't feel like letting Stella off the hook. Sometimes I felt like that was all anybody ever did with Stella. Me included.

It hadn't been up to her to tell!

I wrote back:

Yes.

Then wrote a follow-up that said:

Yes, I am.

I figured that would be the end of it, but then maybe ten minutes later my phone buzzed. Her text said:

Fine. Whatever. I am, too.

17.

Megan was in my seat on the bus the next morning. But some guardian angel must have been looking down on me because the seat beside Naveen was empty. Lou must have been home sick. I slid in next to Naveen, hoping no one would really notice.

"Hey," I said.

"Hey," he said. "Everything okay? Because this is an extreme breach of bus protocol."

"Stella told our dance instructor that I might be moving."

"So you're mad at her."

"Very. I mean, now everyone at dance class knows."

Naveen sighed. "I hate to be the one to point this out, but there is a FOR SALE sign in front of Big Red. It's not exactly a secret."

Of course that was true. I knew Megan had seen it. We just didn't live on a particularly busy street, so I still figured not that many people knew.

"Anyway, even if people know you're moving," Naveen said, "they don't know *why*. If that's what you're worried about."

I nodded. "You always know how to make me feel better."

"Speaking of which, I have materials for you."

I tilted my head. "Dead rodent? Rotting food?"

He shook his head. "For your *dioramas*, Kate."

"Ohhhh," I said.

"I can drop it off later at Big Red?"

"Awesome."

●●●

It was easier to avoid Stella all day than I'd imagined and she wasn't on the bus on the way home. I figured her mom was picking her up to take her to a private session with Miss Emma. Lou, however, was on the bus. So maybe he'd just missed it this morning. I slid into my usual seat alone and was as surprised as anybody when Megan slid into the seat next to me and locked eyes with me.

"What?" I said. She looked like she had something on her mind.

"I heard your parents are selling the house because they're basically broke."

I must have turned as red as Big Red. "Stella told you that?"

"No." Megan shrugged a shoulder. "I heard my parents talking."

I wasn't sure which was worse, Stella having told her or us being the talk of the town. I said, "Next time tell them it's none of their business."

"It's what they do."

"What? Gossip?"

She rolled her eyes. "They're in real estate."

"Well, good for them."

I pushed past her and got off at Big Red, wanting to kick the FOR SALE sign, or maybe throw it into the woods.

I dropped my backpack on the kitchen table and said hi to my dad, who had headphones on at the desk in the loft and told me Mom was out running errands.

"Naveen's dropping by with some stuff for me," I said, and he gave me a thumbs-up.

I went back out to the porch and imagined the bus stopping at Naveen's, and him getting off, and going inside to say hi to his mom, then grabbing a box or bag or filling up his backpack. I sat on one of the chairs on the front porch—which was *not* a rocking chair of yesteryear—and counted cars while I waited for him. I thought maybe eight cars would pass by before he arrived.

His bike came tearing into the driveway after the sixth car passed.

"So whatcha got?" I stood up.

"Lots of good stuff." He had a shopping bag dangling from his handlebars. "At least I think it's good stuff. Take a look."

He held the bag out and we sat on the front porch looking through random pieces of colored foam and fabric and foils and notecards and ribbons and wrapping paper and more. "This is *great* stuff," I said. "Where did you get it?"

"My mom did a big purge of the garage a few days ago but the trash hadn't been collected, so I raided her bags last night."

"Thanks so much, Naveen." There was a small wire pine tree, a tiny disco ball.

"Oh." He reached for the bag as I started putting stuff back in. "This is the best part."

He peered in and moved stuff around and came out with a piece of plastic shaped like a rounded bathtub.

"You've got to be kidding me," I said. "What is it? I mean, what was it?"

"I think it came on a butter dish or something? Part of the packaging?"

"It's perfect." I studied its clear curves. "I'll cover it in masking tape and build the shower rod out of wire, and look!" I dug through the bag and pulled out a square piece of fabric.

"Shower curtain!" Naveen said.

"Exactly! Then I just need to figure out the feet."

Naveen headed toward his bike. "Anyway, I've got to go. I'm behind on homework."

I laughed. "It's *Friday*, Naveen."

"I know, I know. But I don't want to have to do it this weekend." He pushed his bike up toward the road. "Good luck this weekend. With everything!"

"Thanks!"

He took off down the road and I sat there for a while, counting more cars. Wondering where my mom was, which car number would be hers. After eight more cars passed and she still wasn't home I went to the kitchen and found the ivory-colored masking tape in the junk drawer.

It seemed silly at first to be making a diorama of myself in a bathtub, but after a while it didn't feel that way at all.

18.

On Saturday morning, when no one was paying attention, I got a few snack-size Ziplocs out of the pantry and shoved them in my jeans pocket. Then, during another free moment when my mom was in the shower and my dad was in their room sweeping up flies, I took a fork and steak knife out of the cutlery drawer and went out to the composting bin and started slicing up my stink. I'd brought down a handkerchief to tie around my face, and it at least stifled the smell of the chicken zombie rot enough that I didn't feel like I was going to throw up.

I put small pieces of totally gross rotting chicken in each of three bags, then threw the rest into the woods and washed the container out in the stream with apologies to Mother Nature. I'd have to get the bags up into position at the last possible moment and somehow retrieve them after the open house so the house didn't stink all night. It wasn't going to be easy. I had to stay on my toes, looking for any and all opportunities. For the time being, I put the snack bags under a piece of wood in the woodpile under the back porch.

"Where are we even going today?" I asked my mother in the kitchen.

"Horseback riding," she said. "Long pants and boots. And bring a hat."

Excellent.

• • •

When it was time to go, I stepped out onto the porch and smacked my head and said, "Forgot my hat." Bernie was tying a new yellow balloon to the FOR SALE sign, adding a dangling OPEN HOUSE TODAY to two hooks on it.

So I ran inside and downstairs to get the bags, and upstairs to hide the goods—one on top of the bathroom wall, then another on the wall of the closet, and another on the wall of my parents' room. I grabbed my hat, then went back down, all while Bernie was tying that balloon.

"Good to go." I stepped back out onto the porch and put my hat on. "Good luck!" I said as Bernie went inside.

• ● •

My horse was black and white and named Oreo, a name I approved of. As we were being led down a wooded path near a huge barn, I realized I hadn't even named the kittens and how maybe I should. One of them had fur that reminded me of Special K cereal; another had black patches around its eyes like a bandit.

"Stella's going to horse camp to do dressage this summer," I said when my parents' horses started to trot alongside mine in a widening of the path. It felt weird to be talking about Stella when I wasn't talking *to* her.

"That sounds fun," Mom said.

And she actually sounded like she meant it.

"Dressage seems kind of dumb to me," I said.

"I used to ride when I was a girl."

I had the feeling I knew that about her but had forgotten. "Really?"

"Yeah, I always thought I'd have horses when I grew up."

"Oh," my father said. "Give it a rest."

"Not everything is about you!" my mother said.

I had no idea what was going on so I just started talking to the guide who was leading us, asking how old Oreo was, how many horses they kept. Anything to block out my parents.

• • •

When we got home, I realized I'd sort of forgotten *again* about getting the stink *out* of the house. I started to panic when we walked in and found Bernie sitting at the kitchen table. But she just stood up and said a happy "Hello!"

The house didn't smell bad, at all.

In fact, it smelled good.

Fresh.

Better than it had maybe ever.

"How'd it go?" my dad asked.

"Great!" she said.

Somehow my plan had failed. Maybe I hadn't used enough stuff?

"We have some very interested parties at this point," Bernie said. "One woman came alone today but is bringing her husband back with her tomorrow. And a couple from last week is coming back tomorrow, too, for a second look. I'm optimistic. Another developer type showed up right at the end."

"That's great," Dad said.

"All righty, then." Bernie grabbed her bag. "I hope you don't mind. I put a few little Febreze things around."

"Yeah, it smells good," my dad said.

"I can remove them tomorrow. Whatever you like. Toodles." And she was out the door.

"I'm going to the bathroom," I said, and went upstairs to

retrieve the stink baggies. But they weren't there.

Breathing hard, I went to my room and texted Naveen to see if he was around and could meet me at Truxton Pond. I thought about texting Stella but a fight was a fight.

Naveen wrote back, **IN THE MIDDLE OF SOMETHING! COME TO MY HOUSE?**

My parents were sitting out on the back porch with beers on the table in front of them.

"Can I go to Naveen's for a little while?" I asked.

"Are his parents home?" My mom looked at me over her sunglasses.

"Yes."

"Don't be long," she said.

I got my bike out of the barn and took off toward Naveen's. His dad was out front mowing the lawn, and he turned off the mower and waved. "He's around back."

I found Naveen in the backyard with some weird-looking contraption in his hands. He shouted, "Blasting off," then launched an empty, plastic, two-liter soda bottle into the air. It hit a tree and bounced down to the ground, hitting branches along the way.

"Hey," I said.

"Oh, hey," he said.

"This is what you're in the middle of?"

"Come here. I need you to help me pump it up better this time."

He showed me how the bottle launcher worked, and after we'd pumped it up good, we tried again. This time the bottle went really high, but Naveen said, "Still not high enough."

So we tried again, and he made some adjustments to the launcher along the way.

And then, finally, we did two in a row that seemed to meet his goal.

"That one," he said, "was definitely high enough. The problem, of course, is that the aiming isn't precise enough."

"Precise enough for what?"

"To deliver a stink bomb to a chimney."

I nearly gasped. He was doing this for me! But it would never work.

"Naveen," I said. "The chimney has a cap sort of thing on top. A bottle of this size wouldn't fit through even if you had good aim."

"I can't believe I didn't think of that." He nodded. "Okay, so not that useful an invention. But fun at least?"

"Really fun," I said.

We got ready to launch it again.

"So the realtor is on to me," I said.

"What? How?" He let the bottle fly, way high again.

I said, "Woohoo!"

Then: "She didn't say anything, but when we got home, the house smelled like roses, and when I went to get the stink bags, they were gone."

"An interesting twist for sure," he said. "So she didn't tell your parents?"

"No. She left after talking to the three of us. I guess she could have said something then. Or maybe she's going to call them later. Anyway, she acted like everything was normal. Great, even."

"So what are you going to do?" Naveen put the launcher down and sat on the steps to his back porch. "There's another open house tomorrow, right?"

"Twelve to two."

I sat beside him. Maybe it was time to give up. But my grandparents' house was so far away, so dull, so full of parents and grandparents. Dance Nation was still ten weeks away and the thought of the rest of troupe going without me made my stomach tighten and twist. It was still too soon for my parents to find a buyer. I needed at least another couple of weeks so that by the time the whole sale was made official—that had to take at least three weeks?—I'd be in range of a reasonable amount of time to stay behind without them.

"I'm going to have to up my game," I said.

"How?" Naveen asked.

"I have to think."

"Okay, so we think."

We launched the rocket again a few times while we both were thinking. Why else would someone not want to buy a house?

The roar of a truck carrying a huge cylinder full of pesticide shook the air. All the orchards used them, sometimes in the middle of the night. They were the one thing my parents complained about at Big Red. Well, them and Troy.

"I think I've got an idea," I said.

"WHAT?" Naveen shouted.

"EXACTLY!" I screamed.

* * *

We lay in the grass for a while after the noise faded away and made a list of things that made a house noisy.

"Neighbors with leaf blowers," Naveen said.

"Barking dogs," I said.

"Truck traffic."

"Neighbors playing loud music. And fire alarms with low batteries, beeping stuff."

"Yes, there are few things more annoying than constant and unidentified beeping."

"I could figure that out, I think. Like set constant alarms on my phone and hide it somewhere, right?" I took my phone out, and went to the app store and did a search. "Would you believe there is an app for barking dogs?"

"As a matter of fact, I would."

"So I have my phone and we have two iPads," I said.

"You're scheming again! I'm a little scared."

"The *problem* is that I'll be at my grandparents."

"But *I* won't be." Naveen reviewed our list. "And my dad has a leaf blower."

"You're sweet. But I can't exactly ask you to stand around all day with a leaf blower."

"It's only two hours. It's not like I've got a hot date or anything."

I smiled. "I really wish we could have used the bottle launcher."

"Me, too." Naveen sighed.

"I'll text you later?" I said. "When I think it all through?"

He nodded.

•●•

That afternoon, I decided to take Angus for a walk, which I never did, since mostly we let him out to go down to the woods to do his business, but I had to set my plan in motion. I heard music and it was, in fact, coming from the direction of Troy's house. How did his parents stand it?

How did *we*?

I walked up their long, steep driveway.

"Hey," I said, finding Troy by his car with the radio cranked. "Can you do me a favor?"

"Sure, neighbor girl who hasn't spoken to me in five years. Anything you like!"

"Forget it. I was just going to ask you to wash your car tomorrow. Between noon and two. With really loud music playing."

He looked at Angus and came forward to pet him, then looked back at me. "What are you up to?"

"Nothing." I turned to go. "Forget I asked."

"It just so happens I was planning on washing my car tomorrow."

"Really?"

"Really."

"Cool."

Maybe this was going to come together after all.

If I had Troy out blasting music and configured some kind of annoying beep in the house, all I needed was a barking dog and I'd be in pretty good shape—even without Naveen and his leaf blower.

I downloaded the free barking dog app but it wasn't clear if it would time out and just go to sleep. Also, my phone wasn't loud enough to be heard from the house if it was outside. But the old speakers my dad had for his computer upstairs might be. I was pretty sure they were in a desk drawer in the loft. If I plugged them into my phone and set my ring tone to a dog barking, I could just call periodically and voilà, barking dog. I could hide the stuff down by the rocks near the woods easily enough.

Then, when I realized I couldn't exactly call my phone

if I didn't have my phone, I texted Naveen and asked him to call me every ten minutes between noon and two tomorrow, if he could.

He wrote back **No problem** and also said, **I'm charging the leaf blower. Which is battery-powered. I can take a stroll behind the barn for as long as it lasts.**

I wrote back, **<3.**

19.

The ride to my grandparents' house was down a long and boring highway, so luckily I'd only needed one iPad for my noise project. I'd set everything up while my parents showered and put music on in the living room until the second we left to hide the annoying beep I had going every two minutes.

In the car, I asked my parents if I could watch a movie and they agreed, but I had to use headphones so they could talk.

Fine by me.

I watched *Xanadu* and pictured my phone, hidden in the woods just beyond the stream. I hoped it'd be loud enough. I imagined possible buyers standing on the back porch, trying to figure out which neighbor had the barking dog.

I pictured Bernie hearing a beeping sound, every few minutes, thinking it seemed to be coming from underneath the stairs near the napping room, where they'd surely never find the other iPad, which I'd hidden with our Christmas ornaments.

Angus was with us today so I reached over and scratched his head. His breathing seemed shallow, like it did on hot days, and his stomach pulsed with each breath.

I loved my grandparents, I really did. But it was just sort of boring to be around them. They had a lot of stories that they told over and ever. Even when I said things like, "Yes, you've told me about that," they told the story anyway. Maybe that was all you had after a while, after you got old enough that you were retired and then sort of retired, even from being retired. All they really did now was read and play cards with friends and once a year, fly down to Florida to spend a month driving golf carts around some senior community.

The good news was that my grandmother was an awesome cook. And it turned out she made my favorite big Sunday meal, roasted pork. With the best gravy ever.

"So!" she said to me when I was helping her in the kitchen. "How's school?"

"Good," I said. "Fine."

"And you're still dancing?"

"Yup," I said. I wanted to tell her about Dance Nation, but my parents still didn't know I'd signed up.

"It's good to have hobbies," she said.

"I wouldn't exactly call it a hobby. Knitting is a hobby. Fly fishing."

"I just mean it's not like you're going to be a professional dancer when you grow up." She was moving pots and pans around, stirring things. "Teaching is a good job, especially if you want to have a family. Also, engineering. They need women."

"Okay, Grandma. I'll put those on the list."

"It's tough to make a living as an artist these days is all I'm saying. Actually, I guess it always has been. But you probably already know that."

"Yes, *Mom*," my mother said as she wandered into the kitchen. "She's learned that from her dear old mom and dad."

"That's not what I meant," Grandma said. "I just mean that there are choices we make and things we can choose to apply ourselves to, even if we feel like they go against our natural instincts."

"Oh, that's all you meant?"

"Forget I said anything." Grandma was really stirring that gravy now. "Follow your bliss, Kate!"

My mother wandered back out of the kitchen.

Grandma took her apron off and hung it on the hook of a cabinet. "Keep an eye on things in here, okay? Oh, and will you make up a batch of your super-duper salad dressing?"

"Sure."

She left the room and I started getting out ingredients.

The dressing I always made at Grandma's wasn't the healthiest thing in the world, as my mother was always pointing out, but it was definitely yummy. It was basically Russian dressing but made from "scratch" if a bunch of condiments counted as "scratch" and I was pretty sure they didn't. Mayonnaise, ketchup, relish, all mixed up together just right with a dab of Worcester sauce and a dash of hot sauce.

I was just about done when my grandmother came back into the room. She looked like she'd been crying.

"You okay?" I asked.

"Yes, I'm fine. You know how it is." She elbowed me. "Mothers. Daughters."

After our early supper, during which Grandpa told some dopey jokes I'd heard before, like about how Ireland will always be a wealthy country because its capital is always Dublin (ha ha) and how it'll never sink because one of its biggest cities is Cork (groan), I excused myself to go to the bathroom and went upstairs, even though there was a bathroom downstairs. Then I went into the spare bedroom. I lay down on the bed and closed my eyes and tried to imagine us all living here. I just couldn't see it working. For starters, there was only one spare bedroom. They had another room that Grandpa used as a study where I guessed you could throw a sleeping bag on the floor, and I figured that was probably where they'd stick me.

It was a nice enough house. It was just sort of . . . soulless?

I opened my eyes and looked around the room. There were framed photos of my grandparents from trips they'd taken. They looked happy. They still seemed happy. But I wondered if they ever got sad about being old. They were both pretty healthy but there were pill bottles in the bathroom cabinet for sure. Heart pills. Something my grandfather called his memory pill. Once I heard my mom talking to my dad on a drive home from my grandparents' to our house, saying that she'd love for her parents to someday move into the guesthouse so they'd be closer, so she could help take care of them. My dad had joked that my mom was delusional, thinking she'd *actually* want that. Now it was going to happen either way.

Only when I was leaving the room did I see that my mother had put her purse and another bag there. I unzipped it and saw a hairbrush, a few changes of clothes, a book. Her phone was there so I used to it call my phone and imagined it barking in the yard with no one left to hear. I wished I had a way of knowing how it had all gone.

But wait . . .

Why had she brought so much stuff for a day?

Was my mom leaving Dad?

Leaving *us*?

Downstairs, the topic was dessert and everyone being too full to eat it.

"Kate?" my grandmother asked. "How about you? I have cookies."

"Nah." I studied my mother for signs that she was no longer in love with my dad. "I'm good."

"Who's up for a game of cards?" Grandma said. "Maybe gin rummy?"

"It's getting sort of late." My mom looked pointedly at my dad. "Kate has school tomorrow."

Mom went into the downstairs bathroom and Dad and I said our good-byes. Then he said, "Come on, Kate. We'll get the car started."

"Come on, Angus," I said, and he followed me.

I opened the back door for Angus and helped him climb in with a boost. I'd never had to do that before.

In the driver's seat, my dad turned the key and just sat there for a minute, not moving. Just looking at the front door of the house.

"Mom's not coming home with us, is she?" I was watching the door, too. Because maybe now that it was happening, she'd change her mind.

He put the car into gear and started to back out of the driveway, one arm outstretched toward my mother's empty passenger seat.

"No," he said. "She's not. But it's only for a few days. A week, tops."

He stopped at the bottom of the driveway and said, "Want to ride shotgun?"

"I don't have the heart to make Angus move." His head

was on my left thigh.

My father nodded and drove.

"She could have told me," I said. I hated that they had secrets from me.

"She didn't want a scene. She just wants some . . . space."

I stared out the window at the sky, a blue so pale it was almost white as the evening dug in. "Are you getting a divorce?"

"It's nothing like that. Really."

"Then what is it?"

He breathed hard. "Selling the house. It's bringing up a lot of stuff for your mother. For me, too, but more for her. She just needs some time to think about her next steps in life, that sort of thing."

"Is she depressed?"

"We're trying to figure that out. We're trying to figure out if it's just a tough time for us or if it's something deeper. But we're on it, okay? So you don't need to worry. And this, it's just a few nights. I'll probably run up and get her while you're at school one day." He caught my eye in the rearview mirror. "And in the meantime, we get to par-tay."

"Right," I said. "Pizza every night. A total rager."

I put my head back and closed my eyes and was asleep by the time we hit the highway.

20.

"Kate," my dad said, "Kate, we're home."

I climbed out of the car, feeling like I was asleep on my feet, until we got to the front door. My dad had been holding my hand but now dropped it. Angus sat by the door and yawned.

My phone and the speakers were sitting there on the welcome mat, alongside some Ziplocs full of rotting food with a note from Bernie, which my dad read aloud, "We need to talk. Call me ASAP. (Call Kate's phone first, though.)"

He turned to me. "What the heck?"

He probably expected to see confusion but my guess is what he saw was fear. Or shame. Or both. He took his phone out and pulled up my number and called it.

My phone started barking.

And for a second he looked at me like he didn't know me and didn't want to.

"Go to bed, Kate," he said.

I was too sleepy to worry about what would even happen. Maybe I was even relieved I'd gotten caught. And that it was by the realtor and my dad, and that my mom didn't know.

I heard my dad on the phone as I was brushing my teeth and putting pajamas on. It was obviously my mom on the other end. "She slept the whole way. Yeah, we'll be fine. Okay. You, too," he said.

I felt dumb about it all as I drifted off to sleep.

Seriously.

What had I been thinking?

I dreamed that stinkbugs started to crawl out of my closets and drawers and pillows and eyes.

I woke up sweating and thirsty at 1 a.m. and got up to get some water. There was a light on in my parents' room, and I peeked in but my dad wasn't there. So I tiptoed down the stairs, just far enough that I could see him asleep on the couch.

Back upstairs I climbed into their bed, on my mom's side, where it smelled like vanilla, and slept there until morning.

* * *

My father was in the kitchen making coffee.

"Who's been sleeping in my bed?" he said.

"Not you." I reached for my cereal.

He went out to the back porch and sat there with his coffee, not saying a word about the note from the realtor or the bags of stink. I sat with my cereal at the kitchen nook alone for a few minutes then opened the window behind me a crack.

"Dad?"

"Yes?"

"You want fries with that?"

"I'm good," he said flatly, not looking at me.

I got up and dumped my cereal and went out and sat next to him.

"I don't want you to sell the house," I said.

"I don't want to sell it either! But we have to!"

"Why?"

"Because it's the only way we're ever going to get out from under it."

"But I love it here."

"And I do, too. Or I did, until the whole place started feeling like this *crushing weight* on my back. It's not a good way to live." He shook his head. "What were you *thinking*, Kate? You've wasted everyone's time."

"I just wanted to buy some time. To finish out the school year and to make it to Dance Nation."

"I don't even know what that is."

"Everyone in dance class. We're learning a routine to compete in Albany. Stella and I have been wanting this for years. So I signed up. I paid the registration fee. And I forged Mom's signature."

"You should have *come* to us. You should have *talked* about it."

"I tried!"

Didn't I?

He shook his head. "Bernadette told me she had to go across the street to ask Troy to turn his music down and he said you asked him to do it. Did you?"

I nodded.

"You're grounded." He stood up. "For a week. At least."

"But I have dance classes!"

"The point of grounding you isn't to make you happy, Kate." He went inside and came back out with a notepad and pen. "Right now. Letter of apology to Bernadette, whose time you've been wasting spectacularly."

"I'll miss the bus."

"I'm driving you to and from. All week. No bus. And to-day we'll go by the dance studio so you can tell Miss Emma what you did and explain that you will not be competing."

"But, Dad!"

"But nothing!"

I picked up the pen and started writing, then tore off the sheet and handed it to my dad, who read it, then looked up at me. "You were responsible for the smell last weekend, too?"

I nodded.

He shook his head, folded my letter, and put it in his front shirt pocket. "Let's go."

We drove in silence until we got to school. Before I got out, when I had my hand on the handle, I asked, "Are you going to tell Mom?"

"I haven't decided yet."

"Please don't."

"I said I haven't decided yet."

I opened my door and he said, "I'll see you right here at three."

* ● ●

When I walked into homeroom Megan said, "Wow, like, did your dog die?"

Even Stella, who hadn't spoken to me in days, looked concerned. So much so that she came over and said, "Everything okay?"

"I'm grounded," I said.

I flagged Naveen over.

"Grounded?" Stella said. "How long?"

"A week," I said. "Maybe more."

"But my party!" Stella wailed.

"This isn't about you! And what do you care? Aren't we mad at each other?"

She looked shocked. "I'm sorry. I was going to apologize

today. For everything. So I'm sorry. What happened? I want to know."

I nodded. "The realtor found all the stuff I'd left around to sabotage the open house and put it on the front porch for when we got back from my grandparents' last night."

"Your mother must have flipped," Stella said.

"She actually wasn't there. She doesn't know. Hopefully she never will."

Naveen looked confused. So did Stella.

"She's spending a few days with my grandparents." I didn't have the energy to tell them the whole truth. "My grandfather's not feeling great and has a bunch of doctor's appointments she's going along on."

"Oh," Naveen said. "That's too bad. About your grandfather. *And* about getting caught. But even if they get an offer, these things can take a long time. I think?"

"It doesn't matter anymore. I told my dad how the reason I did it was because of Dance Nation, and how I forged my mom's signature. It's all over. He said I have to quit."

"I'm sorry I told Miss Emma," Stella said, after Naveen had gone back to his desk.

"Thanks." It felt good to be talking to her again, even though I was still just a little bit mad. "I'm hoping I can wear my dad down by your party Saturday. Because I want to be there. I really do. I just don't want to have to pick songs out beforehand."

"I get it," she said. "Don't worry about it."

＊＊＊

When I got into the car, my dad said, "How was your day?"

I said, "Fine," but then that seemed to be the end of it.

He drove to the dance studio and parked and was going to get out of the car when I said, "Please? Can I just do it alone?"

He turned the key and opened a window. "Make it quick."

Miss Emma was alone in the studio, doing paperwork at the desk. I could hear the music coming from the tiny dancers class: "Shake, Rattle and Roll."

"I lied about troupe," I said. "My parents never gave me permission."

"Oh, Kate." Miss Emma made a pouty face. "You should've told me! You shouldn't have done that."

"I know," I said. "I'm so sorry. I just really wanted to do it. More than anything. But I have to quit."

"I'm so sorry," she said. "I moved a few times when I was a kid. I know it's not easy, but I know you. You may not like it but you're going to be okay."

"It's not even that we're moving," I said. "It's that we don't even know where we're going. We're going to be staying with my grandparents. It's all messed up."

"I'm so sorry," she said again.

Then she came out from behind the front desk and gave

me a hug and it felt so good that it almost hurt. I couldn't think of the last time my own mother had hugged me like that.

• • •

Dad started driving when I got back into the car but we went left at the diner instead of taking the right toward home.

"Where are we going?"

"Hiking!" He stopped at a light, tapping to the beat of the music with his hands on the steering wheel.

"Dad," I said. "You know I don't 'do' hiking."

"You do today."

"But I have homework to do." I looked out the window. "And aren't I supposed to be grounded?"

"So you'd rather go home and do your homework than go hiking on a beautiful spring afternoon?" he asked.

"Yes."

"Then grounding doesn't seem like a good punishment. If you *want* to be home, then keeping you there is not teaching you a lesson."

"I learned my lesson, Dad."

"We can't go home anyway. Bernadette's there, showing the house to someone who didn't hear the barking dogs or loud music."

"So my plan didn't work after all."

"It wasn't a very good plan, Kate."

I nodded.

We were at a spot I knew well. Minnewaska State Park. My dad parked and grabbed a backpack from the back of the car and handed me a hat. "Let's go," he said. He started up one of the hiking paths with me trailing behind.

It was actually a really nice day. I just didn't much see the point of hiking in general. A bunch of times that I'd been dragged along on hikes, we'd get to the top—some lookout or vista or whatever—and my dad would be all ecstatic, like he'd really accomplished something. I'd just stand there looking out at the view, thinking there was probably someplace we could have driven to see the same view. More quickly, more comfortably, without having to break a sweat.

I was getting winded trying to keep up with Dad, but at least it wasn't buggy out. We probably climbed for about half an hour before we got to a lookout point perched above the lake. There were some mansions across the way. I wondered who was rich enough to live in a house like that. Doctors? Lawyers? Wall Street types? Who?

Maybe my grandmother was right. That it was good to think about practical things, like how you were going to make money in life, enough to support a family if you had one, so that you didn't have to ruin everything and uproot your daughter because you were broke.

Stella and I used to play a game all the time—MASH—
and it told you whether you were going to live in a mansion, apartment, shack, or house, along with what kind of
car you'd drive and how many kids you'd have. We always
thought it was hilarious when we got "shack" and not
"mansion" but what if that's how it all shook out in the end?

"Are we broke?" I asked my dad. "Mom tried to explain it
to me, but . . ."

"Well, we're not rolling in it." He glugged some water
and kept looking out at the lake. He had sunglasses on so
I couldn't really read him. "We still have more than a lot of
people in the world have, Kate. Never forget that."

"I know, I know."

"Anyway, I have a plan," he said. "I just need to be sure
it's going to work out before I tell you . . . Or your mother."

"You have a plan that Mom doesn't even know about."

"I do."

He handed me a bottle of water from the backpack and
I drank the whole thing in one go.

On the drive back home, the setting sun was turning
the whole town pink. And when we turned down one road
that gave you this amazing view of the mountains—all lit
from behind like there was a bonfire in the sky—the world
seemed so big.

Dad pulled into a gas station and parked right near the
quickie mart and said, "I'll be right back."

He left the car running and came back a few minutes later with a pack of cigarettes.

"You really shouldn't smoke," I said.

"I know." He reached into his back pocket, pulled out a lotto ticket, and handed it to me. "Maybe it's our lucky day."

"Please tell me this isn't the plan."

"Oh, ye of little faith," he said.

•••

I did my homework when we got home. Then my dad went out to pick up pizza and didn't take me along, which I figured meant he wanted to smoke in the car without my judging him. After I packed up my backpack for school I called my mom's cell.

She didn't pick up.

After dinner, my dad said, "Hey. You want to hear what I've been working on?"

"Sure."

So we went up to the computer and he turned up the volume on some speakers and unplugged the headset and a song played.

And it was good.

Really good.

It was backgroundy, not like a pop song, and had a cool beat and a neat overall vibe. Like an old record made new by being run through some funky filter. It sounded like the kind of music you'd want blasting out into the yard while friends played boccie. It made me wish we were at a party.

"I love it," I said.

"Really?"

"Yeah, Dad. Really. What's it called?"

"I don't know." He scratched his head. "I've been calling it 'Big Red,' but I'll probably change it."

"Don't. It's perfect. Want to see what *I've* been working on?" I asked, and then I led him downstairs and showed him the dioramas. They were sort of scattered all over the room so I cleared the desk and started to stack them on top of each other.

"Kate, these are amazing."

I hadn't actually realized that I'd almost made the entire house.

"How did you know you could do this?"

"I didn't." I smiled. "Until I did it."

When I went to bed he was still working on the song, sitting at the computer, the only light on in the whole house.

21.

School. Home. Chores. Homework. Sleep. Repeat. It rained for days—April showers for real—so there was thankfully no more hiking. I decided to make a birthday present for Stella so I spent long evenings downstairs working on that. I wasn't sure how long exactly I'd be grounded but figured I'd need a present for her eventually.

I hadn't realized that a full week had passed until I walked into the kitchen and my dad said, "We're running up to get your mom today."

It was Saturday.

Stella's birthday party.

The sun had come out but a few drops clung to my mom's wind chimes out back. Why hadn't he gone to get her during the week?

"Dad," I said, as he was looking for his wallet and car keys on the shelves in the kitchen. "I'm really sorry about what I did."

"Good."

"So . . . Stella's birthday party is today. And this might be the last time I get to go to a party with all my friends and—"

"We have to get your mother, Kate." He opened the front door and Angus stepped out onto the porch and sat there.

"I was thinking I could see if I could go to Stella's house now?" I tried. "Please?"

He breathed out hard. Then he took off his baseball cap and scratched his head. I joined him on the porch, moving a pebble around with my sneaker.

I could feel my heart beating.

He was actually considering it.

"Find out if I can drop you there now," he said. "*While* I think about it. So we know if it's even an option."

I texted Stella. Then stared at the screen and willed her to write back immediately. I didn't have a lot of time.

"It does seem sort of pointless to make you spend all morning in the car." He seemed to be thinking out loud, talking more to himself than to me. "And you *have* been really good about this week, and I *know* you wouldn't ever try to pull a stunt like that again."

I nodded. All true!

Finally, a text came through. **At Main Street Salon, getting hair done. Come here?**

"She said her mom said it's fine and that they're at a hair salon on Main Street." I said it all so fast I almost ran out of breath. I paused to inhale. "Can you drop me there?"

"What do you think your mother would do in this situation?" He squinted at me.

"Honestly, I have no idea."

"Me neither. So I'll take you into town, but here's the condition."

"Anything."

"I won't tell your mother about the nonsense you pulled with Bernadette. But you have to tell her about how you signed up for Dance Nation without our permission."

It wasn't going to be pretty but it wasn't like I had much choice.

"Deal," I said.

"Then let's get a move on."

"I just need to grab a few things." I ran back into the house and grabbed Stella's gift and shoved it in a bag and then got into the car.

It seemed to take forever to get into town. But when we got to the salon, I leaned over and gave him a kiss on the cheek before getting out. "Thanks, Dad," I said.

"Have fun, okay?" He said it in a weird way, like he *really* wanted me to.

• • •

Stella was in a salon chair getting her hair blown out, only it didn't look like her hair. She was loaded up with lavender streaks and looked about three years older than she normally did. She caught eyes with me in the mirror. "What do you think?" she asked.

"I love it," I said.

The stylist spun her around so she was facing me. But he was still drying her hair so she had to shout, "Want to do yours? Maybe a pink streak?"

"Mmmm. I'm not sure."

Hair was whipping around Stella's face. She had to close her eyes and mouth tight. The stylist spun her again and I wandered over to the waiting area and picked up a magazine. It was just pages and pages of hair styles that no one I know would ever have but I kept on flipping and flipping, wishing that my dad had a more fun day ahead of him and wasn't just driving hours to bring home my depressed mother who pretty much blamed him for all their failures as a couple. Part of me felt bad for not going with him, just to keep his mind off things on the drive out. We could have played license plate word games or sung along with the radio. Maybe talked about how we'd spend our lotto winnings.

Stella came over, looking giddy, and grabbed me by both hands. "Your turn."

"I can't."

"My mom says it's her treat," Stella said. "It's temporary!"

"How temporary?"

"Temporary enough!"

"I should ask my mom."

"Come on, they can do you right now."

Stella looked so happy and her hair looked so fun and my dad had said for me to have fun and this felt like a good way to get the ball rolling on that.

"Okay," I said. "I'll do it!"

I got in the chair and the stylist asked me if I wanted a trim while we were at it, so I said sure. My hair had gotten kind of long and uneven and ragged looking. He took a few inches off and I felt like I'd lost five pounds. Then he showed me some color samples and I picked one of the pinks he suggested, and he and Stella decided where the streak should go. She had like ten different small streaks but for some reason everyone thought one would be good for me. So the color went on and it got wrapped in tin foil and then I sat there and waited while a kitchen timer ticked on the vanity in front of me.

"Aaah." Stella was buzzing around the place, getting a little cup of water, and then getting her nails done. I watched her in the mirror. What did it feel like to have everything you wanted? "I'm so excited," she said, coming over and shaking my shoulders.

"Me, too," I said.

"You don't *sound* excited."

"My mom wasn't helping my grandparents," I blurted. "She spent the week with them because she's too depressed and mad to be at the house."

Stella looked like I'd thrown a cup of coffee at her. "I'm really sorry things are so sucky for you right now."

"They should be sucky for you, too!" I said, maybe a little too loudly, but it felt good. "I'm your best friend and I'm leaving!"

"I know," she said. "I mean, *I know.* So let's make today totally awesome, okay? We'll cry another day."

It might have sounded like a ridiculous thing to say coming from someone else.

But coming from Stella—my Stella—right then, it was just want I wanted to hear. It didn't matter that Megan was going to be there or who sang what. What mattered was that it was Stella's birthday and we were together.

"Good plan," I said. "Now let's see what I look like, so we can make bets on how quickly my mother is going to kill me."

Stella laughed and the timer went off and the stylist came and, WOW, that streak in my hair was *really* pink. Since my hair was dark to begin with it sort of looked like the color of raspberries at night. I loved it. My parents would want to chop it off, I was sure of it, but they weren't there and they weren't going to be at the karaoke place, so I decided to enjoy it while it lasted.

We went back to Stella's house and had lunch. I decided to surrender to Stella's will and let her do my makeup as if I were that old Barbie head we'd tortured for so many years.

Stella put on her sparkly blue shift dress and she looked awesome. She looked through her closet and told me to roll my jeans up. She gave me a few tank tops to layer and some bangly jewelry and a pair of ankle boots. I looked like a rocker chick. We both laughed because it was kind of ridiculously not me.

Then I said, "Oh! I almost forgot!" I went and got my bag. I took out her gift and set it atop her dresser. "I made this for you."

It was a diorama of a *Xanadu*-themed roller rink with a tiny Zelda on skates at the center. She studied it for a second and I wasn't sure if she was going to tell me that it was the worst present she'd ever gotten, but then she said, "You *made* this?"

I nodded.

"That is really cool." She moved closer. "She looks just like me."

"I worked really hard on it."

She hugged me. "I love it. You're the best."

The doorbell rang and Stella said, "That'll be Megan."

I groaned. "What is *she* doing here?"

"We're going to do a duet, so we've got to practice a few times."

"Oh. Of course."

Stella went down the hall and came back with Megan. "Oh," Megan said. "Hi."

They put on some song I hadn't heard and started to talk about who was going to sing which parts. Then they started trying to coordinate some dance moves—Megan was hopeless but Stella didn't seem to mind—while I sat on the bed watching with a dumb smile plastered onto my face.

During a spin and clap move, Megan knocked the diorama off Stella's dresser. It was me who picked it up off the floor and put it back on the dresser when we left.

22.

Stella's dad drove us all to the karaoke place since her mom had gone ahead to get the room ready. When we walked in, there were balloons everywhere and a bunch of small tables set up in front of a small stage. I don't know what I'd been expecting—a small room with a monitor, a couple of seats—but I hadn't been picturing this. It was a bar. The back room of a grown-up bar. With a stage and spotlights. Naveen was actually sitting on a high stool at the actual bar, spinning back and forth lazily. He smiled when he saw me. I walked over.

"This place is pretty crazy," he said, over the loud music that had started playing. "You'd never know it from the outside but it's huge."

His hair was slicked back and he was wearing a white T-shirt and dark jeans.

"What's this look you're working?" I asked.

"I have no idea. But I feel like I can sing everything from Bon Jovi to the Four Tops to *Grease* in this get-up."

I laughed. "Yes, it does leave you a lot of wiggle room."

"What's up with the pink hair?"

"It's temporary." I reached up to touch it. It felt the same as the rest of my hair, but *I* felt somehow bolder. I couldn't control much of anything lately but I'd at least taken control of my hair.

People kept arriving and the room filled up. The singing started with Stella, and then it was a blur of laughing and shouting and dancing and singing. I mostly hung back behind the crowd.

My last birthday, in August, Stella and I had gone to a movie and Red Lobster with my mother and two other friends. It had been enough. I wasn't sure it would be this year and I wasn't sure why.

Then Stella came and found me and pulled me up to sing "Girls Just Want to Have Fun" as part of a group that included Megan and two other friends.

Sam Fitch found me getting a drink of water during a break right before cake.

"You were great," he said.

"Oh, thanks," I said. "You, too."

He'd sung a Beatles song and sounded good doing it.

"I like the pink hair," he said.

"Thanks."

But he was too cute. Or too *something*.

I couldn't think of anything else to talk about even though I wanted to.

"I really liked the dioramas you made for Mrs. Nagano's class. I had to redo my essay about which one I liked because it wasn't very good, so when I did it the second time I wrote about one of your dioramas," he said.

"Really?"

"Yup."

"What did you say?" Okay, so this was maybe starting to feel like a crush.

"It's stupid."

"No, tell me. Please." Definitely a crush. Because talking about my diorama with Naveen had never felt like this.

"It was the scooter one. And I wrote about how it made me feel like we're all the star in our own lives. Because it looked like a stage or something. I don't know how to explain."

Then it was time to sing again and I wasn't even sure what had even happened except that all I wanted to do was tell Stella every word of my conversation with Sam so that we could analyze it. Did he like me? What did that even mean?

For a while in there, I forgot all about Big Red and moving

I forgot about my parents, on their way back home in a quiet car.

I forgot about Dance Nation, and how I'd messed up the

troupe routine even though Stella and Miss Emma had both been nice enough not to rub that in my face.

For a while in there, with the disco ball spinning, I was just a girl having fun.

• • •

My dad texted me, asking what time the party was over, and then said he'd be there. I waited outside in the parking lot with the other kids.

"I know it's awkward," Megan said to me. "But I want to get it out in the open."

"I have no idea what you're talking about." Maybe I was a little bit jealous of her duet with Stella.

"No one told you?"

I felt all the fun of the day fading.

"My father's company is buying your house."

I shook my head. "I don't understand."

"It's a thing. He's going to flip it. You fix up a house and turn around and sell it for more money."

"*That's* his career?"

"Yeah." She spotted her ride. "It's kind of awful, right?"

"Kinda," I said, and she walked off.

My dad pulled up and I got in and said, "Where's Mom?"

"Big Red."

"Everything okay?"

"Yes and no." He pulled out onto the street and headed for home. "We have a buyer."

My throat felt suddenly too dry.

"There is some back and forth that typically happens but it looks like a solid offer. It's cash. So it'll be fast."

I swallowed to try to fix my throat and said, "That's great, Dad."

"Let's not get carried away, Kate. It is what it is."

My mom was sitting on the front porch drinking a cup of tea. She put it down and uncurled her legs from under her and got up and gave me a big hug. It somehow didn't feel as good as Miss Emma's had.

"I missed you," she said.

"I missed you, too," I said.

She pulled out of the hug, then reached out for my hair and slid her fingers down my streak. "Is it temporary?"

I nodded.

"How temporary?"

"Temporary enough."

"For who? You? Or me?"

"*Mom*," I groaned. "It was fun, okay. It was fun to do it. And I needed a little fun."

"You paid with your own money?"

"No, Stella's mom said it was a treat and not to worry about it."

Mom turned to go inside, and I followed. In the dining

room, she found her wallet and handed me two twenties. "Take that over there now."

"But—?"

"We're not a charity case, Kate."

I got my bike out of the barn and took off down the road. I wanted to ride and ride and never go back.

23.

Sunday was a quiet day around the house. No one had said anything specific about it, but it seemed like we were all doing the things we most loved to do around the house. I spent an hour on my scooter down on the tennis court, making big circles and doing tricks. My mother sat under the pear tree by the stream with her feet up on an upturned bucket, reading. My father blasted classic rock radio out into the yard and cooked a big dinner out on the grill. We sat out there and talked about hikes we'd gone on where I'd whined the whole time and my parents' honeymoon, where they rode mopeds in Bermuda and my *dad* whined the whole time, and we didn't talk about anything having to do with Big Red at all.

It was warm enough to have a bonfire, so we decided we'd do that, too. My mom had to make a special trip to the supermarket to get everything we needed for s'mores but she seemed happy to go. My dad and I cleaned up dinner while she was gone and it was almost like things were normal again.

When my mom got back, we sat outside in the Adirondack chairs around the fire pit. At first, we didn't even light a fire because the fireflies were coming out, putting on a show. It was like there were a thousand tiny strobe lights in the woods; the crickets seemed to be chirping approval and the frogs croaked, too. The stream was so full and so fast that it was like a roar.

"Kate?" my father said.

I looked at him and he nodded his head at my mom.

So it was time.

"Mom?"

"Yes."

My dad got up and went inside.

"I forged your signature," I said. "So I could sign up for troupe. I didn't want to be the only one who couldn't do it, and I guess I was hoping we'd still be here."

"Oh, Kate," my mother said, and she shook her head, pulled her hoodie closer around her. "There will be other dance classes and other competitions. There's always next year. Seriously, all of this, really, is going to amount to such a *blip* in your life."

I felt my whole body tense. "Dancing *isn't* a blip. *Big Red* wasn't a blip. I've lived here *my whole life.*"

"And when you're my age, you'll have maybe a *handful* of vague memories of what it was like to be twelve."

"That doesn't mean it's not real to me right now!" I was almost screaming. "That it doesn't matter!"

"Of course not."

She was quiet then but everything in my head was loud. We couldn't *live* like this. She could *be* like this.

"I'm going through some . . . stuff," Mom said, and her voice sounded weird. "I'm sorry."

"You need to get help." My voice was shaking. "I need you to get better."

"I know," she said, nodding and sniffling. "I will."

* ● ●

When the light went from the sky, my father lit the fire. I went to find the long pokers we used to toast marsh-mallows, and they were sticky with dust so I washed them.

We continued talking about everything but what was actually going on. I figured my parents knew what the plan was for the house—flipping it—and that they were okay with it, and were doing what they had to do. If they didn't know, I honestly didn't want to be the one to tell them.

I didn't want to think about the week ahead. About having to face Megan at school. And telling Stella that it was really happening. And telling Naveen Big Red was no more. It was all going to be just . . . sad.

Even the excitement I'd first felt when Sam told me he'd written about my scooter diorama had turned sour. I liked a boy. It was possible he liked me. But I was moving so it didn't even matter.

I heard my parents talking quietly down by the fire as I got ready for bed. I knew how the night would go. They'd sit out there and talk until the bulk of the fire went out. Then my mom, sleepy, would drift up to bed and my dad would sit out there, staring at the stars and probably smoking a cigarette until the fire's last embers were nearly dead.

I couldn't sleep.

I got up and went down to the craft room and made a simple diorama, my simplest yet. Just a bonfire. Two chairs. My mom and dad. Gazing up at the stars.

I left it on my mom's night table and went to bed.

24.

A sign that said IN CONTRACT got added to the FOR SALE sign. I didn't understand why they didn't just take the whole thing down already, but it wasn't up to me.

My parents didn't start packing, exactly, but they did seem to do a more ambitious spring cleaning than they'd ever done before. Each item moved or dusted revealed a hibernating stinkbug, or one that was just waking up, and I vacuumed or flushed more of them than I could count Without dance class twice a week—the studio had refunded my troupe fees and class fees—I had a lot of extra time on my hands.

That weekend we had a yard sale. Small pieces of furniture, artwork, a bunch of random rooster things like trivets and creamers. All of it got put out on the driveway for passersby to study and pass judgment on. I felt mortified that my parents were taking nickels and dimes for our junk, and spent the whole time hoping none of my classmates would drive by.

But then Naveen biked over and we snuck off and had ice pops. I filled him in about the rapid end of my dance-troupe career. He told me all about a new bottle-launcher he was building. For smaller bottles. Just for fun. Then we went back and looked at my parents' impressive collection of soup ladles together.

When we were calling it a day, having unloaded most of the furniture and not a lot of the other stuff, a young couple with two little girls stopped by to have a look. They were on the hunt for dollhouse furniture and asked me if we had any. I said, no, that we had nothing like that, and I felt sort of bad about it since the girls looked so disappointed.

Their mom talked to my dad for a while, while I introduced the girls to Angus. The mom said she was sorry they hadn't driven by sooner, maybe seen the FOR SALE sign. They were living in an apartment in Poughkeepsie and had been saving up for a house but hadn't quite started looking.

"I would have bought this place in a second," the mom said, sighing.

"Yeah," Dad said. "It's a great house."

"Where are you moving to?" she asked, probably just thinking she was being friendly.

My dad winked and said, "Oh, you know. On to the next adventure."

I tried to make that my mantra for the next few days:

On to the next adventure!

I started to have elaborate daydreams about what my new school would be like. Maybe it'd have, like, four floors and be all modern and cool. Maybe I'd see some boy across a room and we'd lock eyes and I'd have a new crush just like that. Maybe I'd have some amazing teacher who would introduce me to some subject or book that would change my life and make me want to join the Peace Corps or become an FBI agent.

Anything could happen!

Real estate paperwork came in and my parents signed it. Phone calls to lawyers and agents were made. We started packing and purging and then packing some more. A closing was set for the following week, the first week of May.

My parents talked about possibly homeschooling me through the end of the year and I told them not to be ridiculous.

A moving truck was hired for the closing date, to put our stuff in storage until we knew what our next move would be.

Big Red seemed to know something was happening. I swear it was like it was pulling out all the stops to convince us to stay. The tulips and daffodils seemed to bloom in brighter shades of pink and purple than ever before. The cardinal reclaimed its daily perch out back and sang louder than ever. Forsythia blooms the color of tennis balls appeared down by the court. Pants and her kittens were frolicking every day, wherever you looked. I still hadn't named them and was starting to think maybe it was better not to get attached.

Spring had totally sprung, and the downstairs rooms suddenly seemed dark and dingy. I moved my diorama production to the dining room table. Since I was so close to completing the whole house, I decided to do the kitchen and dining room, and then, finally, the living room.

The small, wiry Christmas tree was one of the few things left in the bag Naveen had given me, so I decided to make my living room diorama a Christmastime scene. I built a fireplace out of cardboard and covered it with gray and black and brown shapes to mimic the stone face. I cut orange and red tissue paper into flame shapes and lit it up. On the other end of the room, I cut windows and placed the Christmas tree in front of it. I didn't think I could make ornaments small enough so I searched around my supplies for tiny beads and strung them on fishing wire, then wound it around the tree. I pulled out a box of our Christmas stuff from under the stairs and grabbed tiny pieces of tinsel and strung them as garland. I raided my mother's wrapping paper and ribbon stash again and found leftover holiday paper, so I made small boxes out of whatever I could and wrapped them, and put them under the tree.

It took me longer than any of the dioramas had so far. I spent a long time with wooden sticks and markers, trying to mimic the wooden beams on the ceiling. I worked in painstaking detail on the butterfly chair so that the pattern and colors were just right. I made mini-parents—one in each chair—and put Angus on the rug at their feet. Then I added myself, lying on the floor looking at the presents. It wasn't based on any specific memory of Christmas, just a general feeling of being how we all ended up on Christmas Eve each year.

I finished it the night before the closing date and decided to show it to my parents. Upstairs, surrounded by boxes, they were pretty much sitting in the exact positions I'd put them in—Angus, too.

"You guys need to get out more," I said. And I turned the box to face them.

My mother took one look at it and started crying.

My dad got up and put a hand on her shoulder and squeezed. "It's really lovely, Kate. Just"—his eyes were filling with tears—"lovely."

Back downstairs I found a large moving box but before packing up, I stacked the shoeboxes carefully, putting each room in its place.

It was my whole life.

In dioramas.

25.

The pink streak in my hair had faded with each passing week, with each passing shampoo, without my really noticing it. And on the day of our move it was gone.

It was a Wednesday—and my parents insisted I go to school. My mother was staying at home to meet the movers and my father was going to the closing. The truck would be loaded by the time I got home and then we'd be on our way. I put my box of dioramas in the trunk of the car, not trusting them to not get crushed in the truck.

I drifted through the day, not really raising my hand in class or talking much beyond the necessary. Sam Fitch told me he was going to miss me and I couldn't look him in the eyes when I said, "Thanks." Mrs. Nagano asked if she could keep my dioramas—and I had to fight hard not to cry.

I thanked a few of my teachers, who wished me well, but I didn't have the energy for a whole day of big, sad farewells. What was the point?

Stella and I rode the bus home side by side in silence. "We'll text and have sleepovers and then we'll apply to the same college," she said, squeezing my hand, but I wasn't convinced any of it would happen.

My mom was sitting on the front steps petting Angus when I walked up. Which seemed like a normal enough scene until I saw that she was crying.

And that Angus was lying there perfectly still.

"I guess Angus didn't want to move either," my mom said without looking at me.

"No," I said. "NO!"

I ran past her and opened the front door so I could run up to my room and throw myself on my bed to cry, but— *bam*—the house was empty.

All the furniture already gone.

All the walls blank.

The chalkboard in the kitchen had been wiped clean.

Everything that showed that we'd ever lived there was gone.

I dropped down to my knees right there in the empty dining room and cried and cried because . . . really, universe? Didn't we have enough to deal with? Hadn't we been messed with enough? Weren't we all already trying so very hard to hold it together?

My father came in and said, "Kate. Come with me."

He'd been out back in the woods, digging a hole. And now he was done.

He'd moved Angus down there and now we were going to bury him.

My mother just stood there in her jeans and white shirt, not talking, not crying—only occasionally lifting a tissue to wipe her nose.

My father struggled to put Angus in the hole and then he started to shovel dirt on top of him. "I seriously"—more dirt—"cannot"—more dirt—"believe this is happening," he said.

I couldn't tell if he was angry or just tired or what. He seemed sort of crazed and maybe we all were.

I started to look around for something to mark the grave with so if I ever came back I'd be able to find this spot, maybe lay some flowers down for Angus.

There was a flat stone down by the pond that seemed like it might do the job. I tried to lift it but it was really dug in. So I kicked it a bunch of times and hurt my foot doing it and I started to cry but now my hands were too dirty to wipe the tears away and then the earth finally let go of its grip on the rock and I carried it over to where my dad was patting his pile. I bent down and lowered the rock and my dad helped me get it settled.

"You were a good dog, Angus," I said.

My mother said, "Well, at least one of us gets to stay."

I wasn't sure what was going to happen then. But I watched as my father looked at my mother, and I guess she shook her head and laughed a little and then he laughed a little, and then he said, "If you'll pardon my French, this has been a—"

"Watch it," my mom said.

The wind kicked up and I heard bells.

"You forgot to pack your wind chimes." I went up to the porch, took them down, and carried them to the car.

• • •

My grandparents met us at the door and came out to help with our bags. I carried my box of dioramas inside and put it in a corner of the living room. My grandmother had made up a bed in the office and I went in there and lay down. She followed me.

"Not the best day of your life," my grandmother said. "But this too shall pass." She smiled. "Hopefully soon, because I'm not sure this house is big enough for me and your mother." She kissed my head. "You, my dear, can stay as long as you like."

I nodded, tears coming out. "I'm really tired." I just wanted her to leave.

"There's clean towels in the bathroom," she said. "Maybe a nice warm soak before bed?"

I nodded again and she got up and went down the hall

and started the water running, then peeked her head back in. "I'll leave you to it."

I went into the bathroom and watched the tub fill and found some liquid bubble bath to use. Voices from downstairs drifted up, echoing in the tub around me once I turned the water off and got in.

"What do you *mean* it's not sold?" That was my mother.

"I couldn't do it." That was my dad. "He was being such a jerk about everything. And I don't know."

"*What* don't you know?"

"I just couldn't do it! What do you want me to say?" He was talking louder now. "I kept picturing Kate and the living room and Christmas, and the idea that this guy was going to make money on our loss, I couldn't do it."

"So *now* what?" My mother again.

"We relist it. We'll find a better buyer."

Then the sound of the front door opening and closing.

I soaked for a while. I imagined Megan's father being so shocked, saying, "But you can't—" and my dad saying, "Oh, yes I can." I pictured my dad leaving the office jittery—terrified of my mom but also kind of pleased with himself. I sank down into the water and smiled with my mouth closed.

After getting out and putting pajamas on, I went downstairs. Through the window I saw my mother on the front porch. My dad was in the living room in an armchair with a baseball game on the TV. My grandparents were tidying up in the kitchen. So I just squeezed next to my dad in his chair and gave him a huge hug.

"You did good," I said.

"Yeah?" he said.

I nodded. "Like, you've got superpowers, good."

"Your mother doesn't think so." He nodded toward where my mother was sitting outside in a rocking chair, not rocking.

"She'll come around," I said, and hoped it was true.

26.

New books, new faces everywhere. New teachers. I couldn't remember anyone's names, and with only six weeks left to the school year, it almost didn't seem worth bothering to try. The feeling seemed mutual. No one—not even teachers or mean girls—is that interested in the new girl when the year's almost over. So I moved through halls like a ghost, mostly undetected, which was the opposite of how things felt at my grandparents' crowded house. Though with Angus gone, even full rooms felt empty. My parents started just disappearing—separately—for hours without any explanation, which meant that my grandmother was home in the afternoon, offering snacks. My grandfather involved me in chores around the house. I read a lot.

"Where's Mom?" I would ask if I came home and her car was gone.

"Just running errands, I suppose," my grandfather would say.

"Where's Dad?" I'd ask.

"Not sure." He'd shrug.

After a while I stopped asking.

I texted Stella, eager for updates about school and troupe, but her texts weren't as fast, weren't as funny. She was already moving on. I knew I should, too. I just didn't know which direction to move in.

I texted Naveen with reports of my boredom and we agreed that we'd both buy and read a book he'd discovered—a novel called *Bear v. Shark*—so we could text about it. One chapter per day.

There were some updates from my dad about Bernie, but they were scattered: "An interested buyer." "A lot of second showings."

But nothing concrete.

My scooter and bike were both on the moving truck in some warehouse somewhere, and I wasn't getting any exercise at all. When I finally asked Grandma if I could move stuff around in the basement, she said sure.

So I went down and moved boxes and tables. It was surprisingly spacious down there, considering how cramped everything upstairs felt. I brought my phone down and plugged it into my dad's computer speakers. A random song in my music library kicked in.

And I started to dance.

Every afternoon after homework and a chapter of *Bear v. Shark.*

One day, "Semi" came on.

I'm passing that old farm again / I carry the same load as the last time.

I slowly moved my arms in graceful arcs, spinning and leaping and sliding and spinning on the floor, the way we did in class.

And maybe because of how my dad and I had talked about it—the longing, the loneliness—it made me feel a little bit better about all the longing and loneliness I was feeling right then.

And my mother's violin part didn't sound as sad as it usually did. It sounded pretty, almost hopeful. Like that sad truck driver was actually going to arrive somewhere and be wanted.

So I hit Repeat and danced to it again.

These tires kick up so much dust.

And again.

Until the sky breaks open wide.

And again.

I drive, it's not a tear.

Again.

That's dust that got in my eye.

I was borrowing moves from probably every video Stella and I had ever watched, moves from every recital dance of the last few years.

After maybe ten times through, I propped my phone on a table with some books holding it in place and hit Record.

Upstairs I got on my dad's laptop and went to the Dance Nation website. The deadline for solo competitors, unaffiliated with any studio, was still a few days away.

I thought about just going ahead and registering, but that hadn't exactly worked out before.

So I opened up an email to Miss Emma called "Solo?" then attached the video of myself dancing and went down to wait for a chance to ask my parents if they'd really forgiven me, if they'd give me this second chance.

• • •

My parents came home sort of happy seeming that evening. I didn't even want to ask why and spoil the good mood. My grandmother had made a roast, and the whole thing felt sort of extravagant for a weekday. I couldn't stop thinking about my email. But Miss Emma hadn't written back yet.

My phone rang after dinner.

"Hello?"

"It's Miss Emma."

I stepped out onto the front porch. "You watched it?"

"Yes."

"Am I crazy?"

"No. But it needs work. And also, the song. Who is it? We need to make sure it's in the catalog of songs you can use without having to pay the songwriter."

"The songwriter's my dad."

"Oh." She laughed. "Then I guess we're fine."

"What do I do?" I said. "I can't afford a choreographer."

"You don't need to. You have me."

"But I don't. You're an hour away."

"Tell me how to find the song and I'm going to fix your routine, add to it, video myself, and send it back to you."

"Oh my gosh, really?"

"Really."

"But Kate?"

"Yes?"

"I need to talk to your parents. I need to know they're on board with this."

My mom had come out on the front porch.

"Can you give me a day?" I said into the phone.

"Everything okay?" my mother whispered.

Miss Emma said, "Sure," and we hung up.

"What's going on?" my mom asked.

"I want to compete in Albany." It felt good to say it out loud.

She almost groaned. "Kate, we've been through his. We simply can't get you to the practices in time. And also, after that nonsense with the forged signature, I just don't think—"

I was shaking my head. "No, not with troupe. As a soloist. I know what I did was wrong, but I'm sorry. And this week, in the basement, I choreographed a routine—sort of—and Miss Emma said she can fix it up for me, make it better. And we can swap videos and she'll critique me."

I sat in one rocking chair and my mother sat in the other. She was eerily quiet.

"I just think it'd be good for me. I feel like I need something to focus on while we're here. For however long we're here."

"You really think you can do it?" she said.

"You could afford to be a little more supportive of me," I snapped.

"I just want to make sure you know how few people make a career out of this."

"I never said I wanted to make a career out of it! It's just something I like to do! I'm not going to end up like you and Dad! Miserable because . . . you know what? I don't even know *why* you guys are so miserable. Because your band didn't become rich and famous? Get over it! What matters is that you did it. That you were *really good* and that you loved doing it."

My voice seemed to echo.

I'd overdone it, said too much.

But she just looked at me. "You're right, Kate. You're absolutely right."

Then we sat in thick silence for a minute.

"And before you storm off," she said, finally. "What I *meant* was is there enough *time to prepare*?"

"Oh." I felt dumb. "If I get started right away."

"Then what are you waiting for?" my mom said.

"Really? You'll drive me to Albany?"

"Of course we will, Kate. It was never about not wanting you to do it. It was about not being able to see how you could."

That night I pictured myself in a diorama—alone onstage with a spotlight trained on me. With my friends rooting me on from the wings. I could see every detail, could practically feel the velvet of the curtain, but I couldn't seem to put Stella in the scene. And then I realized why. It was so obvious. We were going to be competing *against* each other.

Stella would think that was reason enough not to do it.

But not me.

It wasn't about winning for me.

It was about doing.

About stepping out of the shoebox.

• ● •

I got Miss Emma's video and practiced the tweaked routine in Grandma and Grandpa's basement in every free moment I had that week. But I needed more room to spread out, to really move. When I explained this to my mom she said she would figure something out.

By the next day, she'd spoken to my grandfather and then to the people on the board of their little community, and arrangements had been made for me to use the clubhouse for a few hours every afternoon that week and the next.

I only had three weeks to get ready!

There were usually some old people in another room— the library—playing cards or talking but they didn't seem to mind that I was in the common room with all the tables and chairs pushed to the side. There were no mirrors on the wall, which took some getting used to. I had to go with my gut and trust myself from the inside out. After two days of rehearsing on my own, I asked my mom to come with me so we could video the whole thing and send it to Miss Emma for pointers.

"Oh, Kate," she said, when I started the music. "Not *this* song."

"Why not? I love it."

I started it over.

She filmed me.

We did this once, then again, and Miss Emma sounded encouraging. My mother actually did, too. This was the most involvement she'd had in any of my routines—ever—and she morphed into a pretty good dance coach. I had no other feedback coming in so I had to trust that she knew what she was seeing, knew where I looked good and not.

When my mom said she had to drive back to the college for something that weekend—the last one before Dance Nation—I asked if I could come along and try to see Stella. I knew Stella was rehearsing with Miss Emma every Saturday morning so maybe we could meet up after.

Then I had a better idea.

If I could have one actual in-person class with Miss Emma, it would really help.

I could surprise Stella at the studio, and tell her about my solo in person.

So I asked my mom, and she called Miss Emma. And it was set. We'd have to get there early to practice before Stella's session, but my mom agreed.

27.

When "Semi" filled the studio—the very place where I'd *learned* to dance—I felt confident, ready. Like I'd inherited whatever gene had allowed my parents to get onstage and be rock stars even if only for a little while.

"I'm impressed," Miss Emma said when I was done.

"Me, too," my mother said. I hadn't realized she'd been at the door watching.

I did the routine again.

And again.

And Miss Emma told me to do this with that arm and that with this arm, and we worked on a sort of bow/curtsy move that felt natural to me and then we did it all again and again some more.

"Awesome," Miss Emma said, the tenth and last time through.

"Kate?"

I turned. Stella was at the door next to my mom.

"Stella!" I ran and gave her a hug. She felt cold.

"What are you doing here?" She pulled away.

"Surprise!" I said.

"Seriously," Stella said. "What's going on?"

Our moms drifted off to talk and Miss Emma had answered the studio phone.

"I'm doing a solo!" I said. "I mostly choreographed it myself with Miss Emma's help and I've been practicing in my grandparents' basement and—"

"What category?"

She was focusing on the wrong thing.

"Contemporary lyrical," I said.

"That's *my* category."

"I know! Hopefully we can hang out backstage."

Miss Emma ended her call and appeared beside us.

"I didn't know Kate was competing. You know, *against* me."

"I really wish you didn't see it like that," Miss Emma said. "You're all there to do your best. You're not competing against anyone but yourself. And you should be cheering each other on."

Stella just stood there, staring at us for a minute. "I need to go clear my head before my practice."

"Good luck!" I called out as she walked off.

"Stella's just nervous," Miss Emma said, watching her go.

"Send me one more video? Wednesday?"

I nodded, gathered my things, and went to leave but stopped. "I'm sorry you had to reblock the whole troupe routine. Because of me."

"I know you are, Kate," Miss Emma said. "But have you told *them* that?"

28.

My father was making pancakes on Wednesday morning. And whistling.

"*You're* in a good mood," I said.

"I am!" He pointed at a letter on the table. "I sold my 'Big Red' song."

"That's amazing!" I gave him a high five and a hug. "Congratulations, Dad." At the table, I read the letter and said, "Hey, I think I've actually heard of this show!"

"My network debut." My dad turned from the stove and slid some pancakes onto a plate on the table. "*And* . . . we also sold the real Big Red. We have another buyer. We have a new closing date."

I grabbed a pancake that was too hot—"Oh"—I had to put it down.

"Do you remember that woman at the garage sale?" He turned back to pour more batter. "With the two little girls?"

"Sure," I said.

"It's them!"

I pictured those two little girls running around the house, playing in the yard by the weeping willow, tossing flower petals into the stream. I pictured them hiding in the closets in my bedroom and taking a bath together in the claw-foot tub, maybe pretending it was going to walk away and take them to where the wild things are. I imagined they'd start looking for Pants every day like I did; they'd rename her something cute and name the kittens, too.

"I know it's crazy to think about a house that way"—he stopped midflip, with a pancake balanced on the spatula—"to think that Big Red deserved better. But that's how I felt."

"Me, too." I gave him a hug. "But now what?"

"Now I let you and your mother in on the plan." He went about his flipping. "Eat up and get dressed, we've got appointments. Tell your mom."

I laughed. It seemed ridiculous. "What about school?"

"School schmool," he said.

I bolted upstairs and got dressed and woke my mom up and told her Dad had someplace to take us. Then we all had pancakes together.

We drove for about an hour, all the way back toward Big Red, but in town we took some different turns and soon I lost track of where we were. After a bunch of random turns, we pulled into the driveway of a little yellow house sort of set up on a hill. Bernie was standing beside her car, waving and smiling.

"What's *she* doing here?" I asked. I sort of partly blamed her for all of this, which I knew was unfair but I felt it anyway.

"She's the one showing us the houses, Kate."

"We're *looking at houses*?" my mom said.

"Come on," Dad said. "I'll explain later."

We got out and everyone said hi—even me, though I was embarrassed enough to die. Luckily, Bernie didn't seem to be holding a grudge. She took us inside like nothing had ever happened.

"Now," my father said, "you have to really use your imagination on this one. Like imagine the wallpaper gone and the rugs and all."

He'd been here before. He'd been disappearing to look at houses.

We walked in to a small kitchen and I hated everything about it. The color of the cabinets was too dark, all wrong; the floor was a bad yellow; their furniture was like cheap dollhouse furniture that someone had made big. I kept my mouth shut as Dad talked about easy ways to fix various things and followed them into the living room, where brown wall-to-wall carpets covered the floors.

"We'd go back to the hardwood in here," my dad said.

The room was already crowded with the four of us in it.

Upstairs we went into a bedroom and off of that was another room, where there was a crib. It wasn't really big enough to be anything other than a baby's room.

"What would we use this for?" I asked.

My mom shrugged. She seemed about as excited about this house as I was. If we were broke, why were we even looking at houses?

I said, "I'll be outside," and went downstairs and out a back door. There was a yard that was pretty big but it had one tree and no character whatsoever. There was a church as the back neighbor and not even a pretty one.

"So, what did you think?" my dad asked when we got into the car.

"I hated it," I said.

"Not good enough. Explain why."

"I don't know. It just didn't make sense. None of the rooms were the right size. Everything seemed misshapen or shrunken out of proportion. Just bad flow. Bad design."

"I agree completely," my mother said.

"Okay, fine," he said. "But that's the cheapest one by far, just so you know."

Mom said, "For good reason."

"Okay then." My dad reached over and squeezed my mother's knee.

"When did you even do all this?" she asked. "See these houses?"

"When you were, you know, at your . . . appointments."

I hoped that meant what I thought it did.

"On to the next!" he called out his open window to Bernie.

We drove and drove and I kept looking for landmarks I recognized but I wasn't having any luck. "Where are we, exactly?"

"Rosendale," my dad said.

"That's like twenty minutes from home," I said. We'd been to the movie theater there. And to street fairs and farmers' markets.

"Indeed it is."

A few days ago this would have been really exciting. But now I wasn't sure I even cared about being near Stella anymore. Naveen, yes. Miss Emma, of course. But it was all messed up in my mind now. I rested my head back and closed my eyes.

"Here we are," my father said as the car came to a stop a few minutes later.

I opened my eyes.

It was a small red brick house with a white front door and two peaked windows on the second floor. For some reason, it looked like it should be a pediatrician's office, or maybe a bank. I couldn't imagine wanting to live there.

Bernie had arrived first and was standing at the open front door, waving.

I stepped into a living room and dining room area that was more modern than I'd expected from the outside. The paint was all light and bright—barely detectable hues of lavender, maybe, and peach? And the kitchen looked shiny, all new.

Bernie said, "They really did such a nice job with this reno."

It was nice, for sure. Almost too nice, if that makes any sense. Too nice for my parents. Looking at them standing next to that refrigerator, so shiny, and these supersleek cabinets was like looking at two teenagers who'd stumbled into some rich old guy's house.

"Kate?" my dad said. "Thoughts?"

"It's nice," I said. "Almost too nice. I don't understand why we can afford this but not our house."

"It's called a short sale," Dad said. "The owners defaulted on their payments and the bank seized the house so we'd be buying from the bank. The price is way below market value."

"That's depressing," I said. "What happened to them? Where are they going to live?"

"I don't know, Kate," he said. "Right now, these short sales are our only option."

"All of the houses we're looking at are houses other people lost to the bank?"

My dad nodded.

So we were all just part of some weird real estate food chain, looking for our happy ending in someone else's sad tale. It seemed impossible that would ever work out . . . except that it happened that way all the time. People got jobs that other people wanted. People won competitions that other people lost. Some people's bands got famous and other people's didn't. For winners, for losers, for everyone in between, the world just kept on spinning with no rhyme or reason.

We finished the tour, going upstairs to look at three perfectly nice, perfectly lifeless bedrooms, then went out to the backyard and looked at a perfectly landscaped little yard.

"What's the verdict?" my dad asked.

"It's perfect," I said. "Perfectly boring."

"Kate."

"Sorry. But you asked."

"Olivia?" He turned to my mom, who only shrugged.

"I'm sorry, I'm just not feeling it," she said. "And we'd still need a down payment that we don't have."

My dad said, "I've worked out a small loan from Joe."

"Joe?" My mother did not look pleased.

"Yes, Joe. Zero interest. We have a payment plan figured out." Dad sounded more confident than he had in a long time. "And I'm going to be there on weekends for a while, painting and doing yard work and stuff. He's thinking about selling, too, but the place needs work."

Mom just nodded.

"We good?" my father said.

"We're good," she answered.

We all headed toward the car after my parents exchanged a few words with Bernie.

I sighed loudly in the backseat.

"You know what they say," Dad said. "Third time's the charm."

We backed out of the driveway and waited for Bernie to pull out, to lead the way.

29.

As we turned onto a narrow street that curved up and around a stone wall way high, I looked down at the muddy river churning. Dad said, "We're almost there," and my stomach felt like it was churning, too. What if this was going to be my new neighborhood? Was that the same river that ran through town? What if this was the one? What if it was awful? *Then* what?

"It's on this street," my dad said.

"It's cute," my mom said.

It really was.

Back at Big Red, everything felt closed off, like it was our own private hideaway in the woods. Here there were houses sort of on top of each other, with playsets you could see in yards without fences. One house still had some Christmas decorations out front. Another had a sign that said DOG GROOMING and a phone number. The street itself—up and around that bend on the hill, covered in a canopy of trees— felt sort of like a secret place, but it seemed like everyone was just letting it all hang out once you got there. A woman walking a dog gave our car a friendly wave as my dad slowed down, then we pulled into a driveway where Bernie's car sat.

"There she is," my father said with some fanfare.

I almost smiled. It looked a little bit like a gingerbread house, only gray instead of cookie-colored. It had a red front door and a chimney and a big arched window with white trim on the top floor. The front yard was a long stretch of bright green grass with a garden and a white wishing well.

"It's cute," my mother said. "Is there a backyard?"

There didn't appear to be. Behind it there seemed to be nothing but a big hill made of rock.

"There's a deck area, but no, not really." My dad got out of the car. "There's this front yard, though."

"But everyone can see the front yard," my mother said as she got out.

"Can we please keep an open mind, here?" my dad said.

"Sorry," Mom said.

Bernie came out of the garage with a set of keys in her hands. "I think you're going to like this one, Kate."

"I really hope so."

She led the way for me, and my parents followed.

Inside the front door was a tiny living room and dining room area—already emptied of furniture—with sliding glass doors leading to a patio off to the side. There was a small coal-burning stove with a fire lit in it and a chimney that ran up the wall and out the front of the house. I couldn't think of where all our furniture would go since the place was so small, but it was cozy seeming, not cramped.

The kitchen was right there, separated from the living room by an island with a wall cutout. The cabinets were country-ish, painted a pale blue. There was a closet and laundry room down a hall and a small bathroom and that was all for that floor.

Up we went, to a second floor with a big open room at the top of the stairs, and then two small bedrooms.

"One of these would be an office," my dad said. "But you'd basically have this floor as a suite. You'd have this bedroom and then this room at the top of the stairs for whatever you wanted. Like your craft stuff or whatever."

The windows were huge and looked out in two directions, making the room feel light and bright. The yellow of the walls was perfect, like warm butter, and the trim was all newly painted white.

"Where's all their stuff?" I asked. "Why are they already gone?"

"I don't know, Kate," Bernie said. "It's not really the kind of information we share."

• ● •

Out the front window I saw a boy around my age riding his bike down the street, being chased by a shiny, happy black dog.

"Come on," my dad said. "There's one more floor."

Upstairs, there was a master bedroom at the front and then a huge bathroom at the back. In between there were two closets, his and hers. There was also a door by the stairs that went out onto a deck on the side of the house. Stepping out onto the wooden slats, I could easily see my parents sitting there together late into the evening, or with morning coffee and a book.

"Cute," I said.

Then we went back down a level again and out another door to a deck out back, this one larger. From there you could see the rocks that made the wall behind the house and how big they were. I imagined in the winter there'd be icicles hanging off them.

At least I hoped there would be.

That was the kind of stuff they should put in real estate listings. Not how many bedrooms there were or what the floors were made of; that was all stuff you could see for yourself once you got there. They should tell you whether there were icicles or cats who came by to say hi or cows that mooed you awake. They should say things like "Beware:

Mean Girl Next Door," or "Stinkbugs Love This Place" or how there was a great pond just beyond the neighbor's house that was perfect for skimming rocks. People selling houses should have to write all that stuff down for you so you'd *know* whether any of the wishes that had been wished into the well out front of the house had come true.

My parents and Bernie were gathered in the living room when I went back inside.

"So?" Bernie asked. "What do you think?"

The whole house was a *little* bit buttoned up for my parents, but maybe that was a good thing. Maybe this house would help them focus. Also, there was no napping room. That seemed like a good thing. Though I guess my mother hadn't actually taken a nap or gone upstairs at my grandparents' to lie down in weeks.

"It feels like a dollhouse," I said, finally, and they all just looked at me. "I sort of love it."

Everyone seemed to breathe out this huge sigh of relief. It was like the room actually got more full with air.

"But there's no backyard," my mother said.

"But there's a front yard," my dad said. "And all the neighbors seem very nice."

We went out the sliding doors and onto a side deck.

"Kate?" my mom said. "You're okay? No backyard?"

I thought about all the stuff we'd done in the yard at Big Red. Boccie and croquet and badminton. I remembered the parties with people splayed out in the yard here and there and everywhere. I felt sad about my stream. And Pants. And the kittens. And Angus. But all of that was already gone.

I gestured to a long path of grass. "That's a pretty good spot for boccie right there."

We all were quiet for a while and then my dad said, "Liv? It's pretty much the best we're going to do. I've been all over the whole Hudson Valley and I really think this is the one."

Bernie drifted back into the house.

"It really is cute." My mother looked up and down the block. "I sort of wish it was all a bit more spread out but . . ."

We just waited.

"I think I might love it," she said.

My dad said and I both said, "Yes!" and he hugged her and they looked happier than they had in a long time.

Bernie poked her head out. "Does that mean we're making an offer?"

Dad said, "Yes."

And Bernie said, "Now I have to remind you, these short sales can be quick or drawn out and there's no guarantee."

My dad said he understood, though I didn't.

He and Bernie went to talk about some paperwork and my mom and I sat on the edge of the deck.

"Hey, Mom?"

"Yeah?"

"What are your appointments for?"

"Apparently I am having a textbook midlife crisis," she said. "But I'm seeing a therapist and it's getting better by the day. Talking helps."

"Good," I said. "I'm glad."

My dad called my mom over so we got up. They needed my mother's signature on a few things. Meanwhile, the boy on his bike was back, with his dog. Both of them moving more slowly this time.

"Hey!" he called out when I caught his eye.

"Hey." I walked down to the end of the driveway where he'd come to a halt, straddling his bike. The dog sniffed my sneakers and happily ran around in circles then came back to me. I bent to pet him and scratched him behind the ears.

"You buying this house?" He had light brown hair that was too long in front of his eyes and he pushed it over to one side with his hand.

"I think so," I said. "This may sound like a stupid question, but we've been all over the place today. Where are we, exactly? What town?"

"Lloydville," he said.

"Which is . . . where, exactly?" I knew the name, but couldn't place it.

"The Wallkill River is that way. And New Paltz is that way. Frosty Fest is just over there."

"How far?" I asked, bracing myself for the answer. We'd been to Frosty Fest, a holiday light show, every year for as long as I could remember.

"Ten minutes?"

"So how far from New Paltz?"

He shrugged. "Twenty minutes, give or take."

"So what high school will you go to?" I asked.

"My brother goes to Highland."

"Wow. That's where all my friends will end up, too."

"So that's a good thing. Right?"

"Yeah, mostly!"

I'd be in school with Naveen again!

And Megan. And Stella.

In the meantime, I could study with Miss Emma.

I could compete with the troupe next year!

"Any more questions?" he said.

"Just one. Who lived here? Where did they go?"

"That's two."

"Okay, *two* questions." I smiled. "Jerk."

"They were an older couple and after the miserable winter they decided to unload this place and move permanently to their place in Florida."

I wasn't sure I understood exactly how you could do that, just "unload" a house, but at the very least it sounded like they weren't bankrupt or homeless.

He put a foot on a pedal. "Well, if it works out—the house—we'll hang."

"Sounds like a plan," I said.

Then he whistled. "Oscar! Come on, let's go!" And he pushed off down the street and Oscar followed. Right away he circled back. "Hey, what's your name?"

"Kate."

"I'm Benny. See ya."

I watched as he rode off and then up a driveway a few houses down, across the street. He laid his bike down on the blacktop and walked inside, holding the door open for Oscar.

"Look at you," my mother said. "Making friends already."

"Let's not get carried away." I was very much eager to get home so I could dance the rest of the day—the week—away.

But I very much liked the idea of hanging with Benny.

"Us?" She slid her sunglasses onto her face. "Never."

"Can we get another dog?" I asked. It was like I could feel the ghost of Angus, licking my palm.

"First things first."

30.

I **couldn't sleep the night** before the competition and I woke up *way* too early the morning of it. After a quick shower I went to the kitchen but had a hard time thinking of anything I wanted to eat. I forced down a piece of toast and grabbed a few granola bars and shoved them in my bag. Then I went back upstairs to do my hair. Which was sort of pointless. I wasn't any good at it. I was about to text Stella to ask if she thought her mom could do my bun later but maybe that wouldn't be the best idea.

We hadn't spoken all week but I'd gotten texts from Madison and Nora, who wrote, **Heard you are doing solo!** and **Break a leg!**

I wrote back to apologize that they'd had to reblock their whole routine because of me. The fact that they'd both forgiven me seconds later only made me sadder that I wasn't dancing with them. What if they bombed or choked?

What if *I* did?

What if *Stella* did?

Would she even *let* me apologize?

"You ready?" My dad entered the room looking barely awake, my mother on his heels.

I nodded.

When we got to the car my mother took the keys from him and said, "I got this. You're still half-asleep."

I played "Semi" over and over again with headphones on, running through my routine in my head. I wasn't sure I'd ever listened to it while on the road and it felt somehow right to be listening to lyrics like, *It's raining / It's pouring/ Got sixteen miles till morning*, while the world whipped past in a blur of lines.

After a nap, my father declared he was starving and needed coffee and I was actually finally feeling hungry, so we went through a drive-through and loaded up. I had a Coke, which I only ever really had at fast-food places, and it really pepped me up.

The one-and-a-half-hour drive seemed endless—the world waking up around us, the traffic thickening—until we were there and it felt too soon.

* * *

There were dancers everywhere at the conference center, all dolled up in sequins and tutus. I'd opted, at Miss Emma's suggestion, to just wear a black leotard with a squared-off, boy-short sort of cut. I felt a little plain alongside the others, but I felt like me.

We found the registration desk and searched for the dressing area I'd been assigned, glimpsing a peek of the main stage on the way. It looked huge from the back of the hall. I felt like I might throw up.

My dad was flipping through the program and looked up. "You're dancing to 'Semi'?"

"I thought you knew." I hadn't been hiding it.

He shook his head, kissed me on the forehead hard.

Then we found my dressing area, where a ton of other girls were pacing and warming up, then we found Miss Emma.

"How are you feeling?" she said, taking me by the shoulders.

"Good, I think."

"You look great. But wait. Come with me. Let's fix your hair."

She sat me in a chair in front of a mirror and my parents came over and Miss Emma said, "So, Mr. Marino, you're like a rock star, huh?"

My dad smiled. "You're hired."

"That's my mom on violin," I said. "I don't think I told you that."

"You didn't!" Miss Emma said. "That's amazing."

An announcement was made, asking nondancers to leave. So my mom kissed me on the cheek and squeezed my hand. "We're already so, so proud of you," she said.

I pressed away tears so as not to mess up the little makeup I'd put on.

"Break a leg, Kate," my dad said, and they were gone.

Miss Emma started to redo my bun.

"Where's Stella?" I dared.

"She's freaking out over there somewhere." She was holding a bobby pin in her teeth. "Apologize yet?"

"To Stella, no. I wanted to do it in person."

Miss Emma spun me around and smiled. "Well, then hop to it."

• • •

Music surged into the air around us. Lights shone like kaleidoscopes behind curtains. Names started being announced through an echoey microphone. Bodies shuffled this way and that. Soon I was alongside Stella, waiting for my turn. Or hers.

"I'm sorry about troupe and making you guys have to relearn everything," I said. "I hope you guys do great."

She tilted her head and light caught the glitter speckled on her cheeks. "Thanks." She shook her arms out and looked off toward the stage. "Honestly, solo competition is way more important to me, anyway."

I was going to say something else—maybe just "break a leg"—but then too quickly, it was my name being called and I was there, center stage.

I couldn't make out any faces in the crowd—a packed auditorium—but I didn't have time to anyway.

I heard the opening guitar and keyboard bits of "Semi."

I felt so grateful for Miss Emma and for music and for my body and for my dad, who had superpowers like finding a house we could afford, and for my mom and the stuff she was going through, even though it didn't make her the most pleasant person to be around right now.

I imagined them watching me, maybe feeling sad about the good old days and also thinking how different I was from them and yet still such a part of them.

I saw the whole of the stage as a diorama, with me at the center, with a spotlight shining on me, maybe for the first time in my life. Maybe for the last. Who even knew?

And then it was done.

And there was applause, and when I took a bow, I felt like we didn't even have to stick around for the scores, the results.

I'd done it.

That was the thing that mattered.

31.

We waited and waited, days upon days, for the phone to ring, for it to be Bernadette with news. I even started think of her as that, Bernadette, in order to up the good karma. There was paperwork and more paperwork coming and going and my father had a few appointments related to the house stuff but mostly I was living in a vacuum of information.

I spent a lot of time watching the video of my "Semi" dance, which had taken seventh place in a group of fifteen. Stella, who'd taken third place, had come over to congratulate me after the competition.

"You did great," she said. "I'm happy for you."

"You're only happy for me now that you did better than me," I said.

She looked a little bit mad, or stunned. "I don't know how I got this way."

"Well, we have to figure out how to fix it," I said. "Because there's a *possibility* my parents are buying a small house near Big Red. So there's a *possibility* I'm coming back to Miss Emma's classes. And we can't be like this."

She nodded. Then smiled. "You might really be moving back?"

I nodded.

"That would be amazing. Truth is, I've been miserable without you." She leaned into me. "Not as miserable as your boyfriends Naveen and Sam, but miserable."

"Quit it," I said but it didn't really bother me. Not like it used to.

● ● ●

On Tuesday of that week my grandmother came home with a pair of new shoes, and she left the empty box sitting on the living room floor.

I was watching something random on TV but the box just kept calling to me.

It had been weeks since I'd made a diorama, and I missed it.

"Hey, Grandma." I found her in the kitchen. "Do you have any craft stuff? Construction paper? Ribbons? That kind of thing?"

"There's a box of stuff in the office closet but it's not much."

"Can I look?"

"Sure."

I left then popped my head back in and held up the empty shoebox. "Can I have this?"

"Knock yourself out," she said.

I went up to the office and looked around in the closet and found the box. There was more good stuff in there than I'd expected. Some gift bags from various parties and holidays. Colored tissue paper. Old greeting cards and ribbons.

I opted to do a tall diorama. I lined the three back walls with blue paper, like the sky, then put green down on the bottom for grass. I took the shoebox lid—made of white cardboard—and cut a few rectangles and triangles, then colored them with gray markers, after drawing some windows and doors. When the ink dried, I set about taping them together to form the shape of a house. Using more cardboard, I made a circular roll, then went downstairs and got some toothpicks from the kitchen cabinet. I used them to prop up a small "roof" for the wishing well.

Lastly, I made a little me, a little mom, and little dad.

I put us out on the front lawn with some boccie balls of Play-Doh around us.

The whole thing felt cramped. Too small.

Life was bigger than a shoebox.

It had to be.

So I took a pair of scissors and cut open the box, folded out all the sides so that the house stood on a flat piece of cardboard.

It was a wish sent out to the universe, a wish that we were open to anything.

•••

We gathered around the TV together that night. Dad's song "Big Red" was going to be making its network debut. My mom made popcorn and we watched and waited and waited.

A half an hour in, during a montage of people doing things with machines and test tubes and swabs in a lab, the song came on and my dad turned the volume up and stood and reached out for my mom's hand and then mine and he pulled us off the couch and we all danced until the montage ended and the song faded out.

"Excellent." My mom kissed my dad. "Congratulations."

"So are we loaded now?" I asked. I knew the check had arrived in the mail that day.

"Oh sure," my dad said. "Absolutely rolling in it."

"I think there might be *just enough* room out front for a tennis court," my mom said, and they laughed. And I finally got the joke. I laughed, too.

32.

I was giddy two weeks later, watching the movers
unload our stuff at the little gray house. Benny came by to
say hi and sat out front with me while our furniture got
unloaded. It felt like seeing old friends. Our couch. The dining
room table. My beanbag chair!

"I did something pretty crazy," I said to Benny.

"Yeah?"

"I tried to sabotage the sale of our old house by hiding
cow turd in that beanbag chair."

He laughed. "I'll be sure to avoid sitting on it then."

"I took it out."

"Still."

The movers took dining room table chairs off the truck.

"I guess you really didn't want to move, huh?"

"It was the only house I'd ever lived in, so, yeah. I loved it."

"This place is pretty cool." He nodded his head back toward the house behind us.

"Yes," I said. "Yes, it is."

• • •

A week or so later, I was rearranging the furniture in my room, trying to get it just right, when the doorbell rang. "Kate, can you get that?" my mom called out. "My hands are covered in chicken juice."

Gross, I muttered as I ran down the stairs—having some flashbacks to my Tupperware of stink—and then opened the door.

"SURPRISE!" shouted Naveen and Stella.

I squealed and went to hug them both. "What are you guys doing here?"

"Your mom invited us," Stella said, presenting a tray. "I brought brownies."

"And *I* brought my bottle launcher," Naveen said.

"Awesome," I said.

My mom came to the door and said hi and went out to talk to Stella's mom by her car.

"Come in," I said. "Let me show you around."

I gave them the tour of the house and they said they thought it was great and then we went out onto the front lawn, where Naveen had left the bottle launcher. My mom came out with a picnic blanket and some tuna salad sandwiches and drinks and we sat and ate and everything felt normal again.

Naveen got up to load the launcher just as Benny skateboarded past.

"Hey, Benny!" I called out.

"Hey!" He hopped off his board, picked it up, and came down the driveway and into the yard to join us.

"These are my friends Stella and Naveen," I said. "This is Benny."

"How high does that thing get?" he asked Naveen.

"Highest it's gone so far is probably thirty feet," Naveen started pumping it up and Benny got up to help hold it. Then Naveen said, "This is going to be epic," and he let the bottle fly and we all watched it go up and up and up and up, and if it wasn't way past thirty feet high, it sure seemed like it was.

"That is awesome," Benny said.

"Truly," I said.

"Nailed it," Naveen said, high-fiving me.

Stella lay back on the picnic blanket and said, "You guys are weird but I love you anyway," just as the bottle landed on her stomach with a hollow *thwack*.

We all laughed and lay there talking about nothing much.

But I still felt like the air was too quiet. "I'll be right back," I said.

Inside, I looked around on the kitchen counter for the car keys, then went out and opened the back passenger side door and slid my mother's wind chimes out from under the front seat.

They clanged and sang as I closed the door and walked them over to the front deck and looked around for a hook to hang them on.

My father's car pulled into the driveway and he got out and came over and said hi to everyone.

Then, looking at me, he said, "I'll get my tool kit."

He and my mom came back out of the house together a few minutes later and we found a spot where the side of the house had a little overhang. My dad hit a nail in and I hooked the chimes on. The green stone seemed to light up. The wind blew approval.

● ● ●

After Benny took off down the street, saying "Catch you later," Stella and I just stood in the front yard for a minute.

"He's cute," Stella said.

"No, he's not," I said. Then I counted to five. "He's *really* cute . . . and he's mine."

"If you insist," Stella said, and we both smiled and went inside to watch our dance videos.

• • •

Mrs. Nagano seemed happy to see me when I went back for the last week of school. We were clearing out the classroom so it was time to take our dioramas home. I took both of mine to my desk and studied them.

Me and Pants and the kittens first. I wondered how they were doing. Whether Pants even missed me. I wondered whether the new girls had come up with good names like Special K and Bandit.

Then I looked at the scooter diorama, the most thrown-together of all the ones I'd made. It suddenly seemed silly to me that I was so into scootering in circles in my own backyard. Now I had a whole quiet street to ride up and down on.

Across the room, I saw Sam packing up his walkway diorama. He smiled at me but I didn't feel swoony when I smiled back. Maybe because I'd been gone for a while. Maybe because of Benny, some of the magic was gone.

Naveen was boxing up his shark and bear diorama and I caught his eye. "So did you ever decide? Shark or bear?"

"I have absolutely decided, Kate—" He smiled wide. "That it really could go either way."

I laughed and wondered when Naveen would start thinking of girls as, well, girls.

I wondered whether he'd ever have a crush on me, or

whether I'd approve of whoever he chose.

I was happy that my parents decided to let me finish middle school there in my old school—driving me to and from for one whole year—but also felt like it wouldn't have been the end of the world if I'd had to go to school with Benny and the other kids from the neighborhood.

● ● ●

We went out to dinner with Stella's family as a sort of end-of-school celebration and got home late. I went up to get ready for bed and stopped to put my first two dioramas with the others, all stacked in the upstairs den. Looking at my weeping willow made of string, I thought about branches that die off and fall away.

I wasn't sure I'd ever make another diorama.

What would I dream up next?

I turned the light off, and out the window, fireflies pulsed in time with my heart.

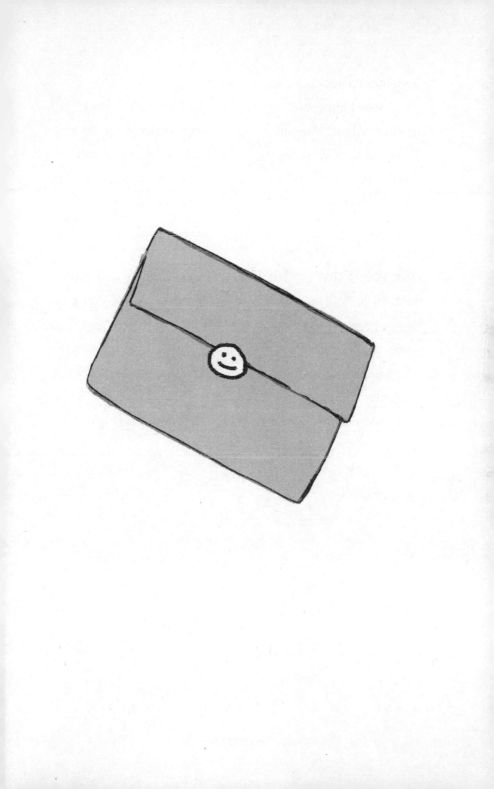

Kate Marino
Lloydville, NY
"Big Red"
aka 74 Trescott Road
Highland, NY
ATTENTION: The two girls that live there now!

Hi!

You don't know me, but I lived in your house for a really, really long time. My whole life, up until just a few months ago.

There are a few things I thought you should know.

That cat that hangs around the barn and the yard is named Pants. Named by me, I mean. Because she looks like she's wearing pants. But you probably figured that out. You can change her name if you want to, like if you had your heart set on some other name. But Pants has been her name for a long time. She had kittens right at the end of winter but I never named them. Maybe you already have.

In the fall, you might want to tape around the screen doors in some of the old windows. Otherwise stink-bugs are just going to waltz in every crevice. They're dumb. But also: Gross.

There's a dog buried in the woods just past the stream. His name was Angus and we put a big rock on top of his grave. I hope that doesn't freak you out, but he lived here as long as I did and we couldn't bear to put him anywhere else. If you grow up to be handy with a chisel, maybe you'll carve his name into that rock. Or maybe you'll leave him a flower once in a while.

The cows next door are pretty annoying; you've

probably figured that out by now. *Moo!*

We have no idea why there are so many dead flies in the master bedroom. So good luck with that.

Speaking of which, my friend Stella lives right around the corner from you. Maybe your parents will ask her to babysit you guys when she's a little older? She is awesome at a lot of things, like dancing. She's also just fun to be around except when she gets a LITTLE too competitive and has to be told to calm the heck down because it's just a dance competition and anyway I CAME IN SEVENTH SO YOU DIDN'T REALLY HAVE TO WORRY!

Also fun: Naveen. You'll see him riding his bike or maybe launching soda bottles into the air. If you ever need help, basically with a problem of any kind, he's your man.

I hope you're not sad about leaving whatever place you were living in before. Our new house is smaller, but I like it. I miss seeing Pants around, especially now that Angus is in dog heaven, but my parents say that maybe we'll think about getting another dog when we're settled. Meanwhile, I've made some friends, like this guy Benny who is sort of hilarious, and the funny thing is I'm not even that far away from you. I'm actually going to end up at the same high school as all my old friends and I go to the same dancing school I was in last year.

Here's the thing. Change is hard. Until it's not.

Trust me. One day, you'll end up leaving Big Red, too. (Oh, yeah. We called it Big Red.) Hopefully it'll be because you won the lotto and are moving into a seaside mansion. Or maybe just because you're old enough that you're going away to college.

Either way, I bet you'll be sad about leaving. Which means that for the time being you should kick back and enjoy. Maybe go scooter around on the tennis court that isn't really a tennis court. (Long story.)

One last thing. There's a bag with a dirty spatula in it down by the woods. You can see it from the path up to the road. Throw it out if you can. Then go wash your hands. Thanks!

Oh, and you guys totally need to get some wind chimes to hang on the back porch. There's a hook there, just waiting. . . .

—Kate

ACKNOWLEDGMENTS

Lisa Cheng, you're the best. I may make fun of you a wee bit ("Pick! Pick! Pick!") but I deeply appreciate your attention to detail and your obvious love of stories, books, and the job of editing them.

I am so grateful to be working with the amazing Running Press Kids/Perseus team:

Chris Navratil, Allison Devlin, Valerie Howlett, Frances Soo Ping Chow, Stacy Schuck, Geri DiTella, Elenita Chmilowski, Susan McConnell, Liz Tzetzo and, of course, T.L. Bonaddio. We should hang out more.

Thanks, always, to David Dunton at Harvey Klinger agency.

That goes for you, too, Nick Altebrando.